CIRCUS OF THIEVES

ON THE RAMPAGE

WILLIAM SUTCLIFFE

ILLUSTRATED BY DAVID TAZZYMAN

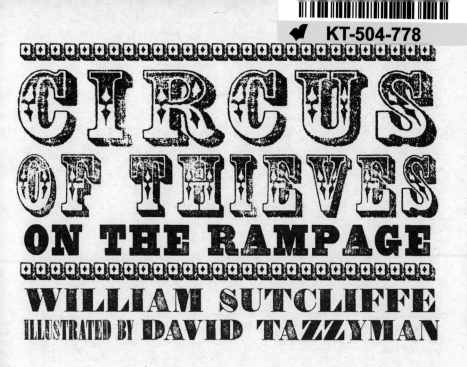

First published in Great Britain in 2015 by Simon and Schuster UK Ltd
A CBS COMPANY

Text copyright © 2015 William Sutcliffe
Illustrations copyright © 2015 David Tazzyman

1 3 5 7 9 10 8 6 4 2

Simon & Schuster UK Ltd
1st Floor, 222 Gray's Inn Road
London
WC1X 8HB

Simon & Schuster Australia, Sydney
Simon & Schuster India, New Delhi

A CIP catalogue record for this book is available from the British Library.

PB ISBN 978-1-47112-025-1
eBook ISBN 978-1-47112-026-8

Printed and bound by CPI Group (UK) Ltd, Croydon, CR0 4YY

www.simonandschuster.co.uk
www.simonandschuster.com.au

For my three rampagers:
Saul, Iris and Juno — WS

For Daisy & Theo — DT

Just one more bath

LET US BEGIN WITH A LEAF. Not a green leaf, but a brown one, curling up at the edges, clinging on by a feeble, sad little dried-up stalk. Yes, folks, it was autumn – the time of year when leaves have had enough of being leafy and pretty and green, and decide all at once to shrivel up and dive-bomb into the mud. We all get the urge to dive-bomb into mud from time to time, but leaves are very good at waiting until mud is at its soggiest and squelchiest, probably because they know they only get one dive.

This particular leaf – let's call him Kevin – had his eye on a deep, pungent, cow-patty puddle directly beneath the branch where he'd been hanging all summer. He'd been watching this puddle ripen for more than two weeks. When he decided it was time to take the plunge, he yelled out, 'GERONIMOOOOOOOO!' and went for it, shrugging himself free of Old Branchy and fluttering downwards.

This was the high point of his year.

'Bye-bye, Branchy,' he hollered. 'To be honest, I never really liked you anyway!'

Sadly for Kevin, a gust of wind came up at that exact moment and blew him off course. This may have been divine punishment for his ingratitude and rudeness, or perhaps it was just a coincidence. It didn't blow him far, but this was no ordinary field, and Kevin was dismayed to find himself landing not in a lovely, cold, murky, composty, dank puddle, but in a hot, soapy, clean-as-a-just-cleaned-whistle, lavender-scented bubble bath. Yes, he fell from his tree, as leaves always do in autumn, and he landed in a bath, as leaves, on the whole, don't.

How on earth could a disaster of this kind befall an innocent, filth-loving leaf such as Kevin?

How is that even possible?

I've never heard such nonsense in all my life! What a load of absolute tripe!

Take a deep breath. Calm down. And allow me to explain.

The cause of Kevin's soapy demise was an outdoor bath belonging to the internationally renowned, semi-retired and deeply fragrant trapeze artist, Queenie Bombazine.

Queenie loved to bathe. It was her favourite activity. She also loved fresh air. Most people with two incompatible enthusiasms of this sort would have been happy to bathe, then go for a walk, or vice versa, but Queenie Bombazine was not most people. She was Queenie Bombazine, circus legend, aerialiste supreme, Mermaid of the Skies (but we'll come to that later).

So – and it's not that strange; in fact, it's surprising more people don't do it – Queenie Bombazine had hired a plumber to run some water pipes into the field behind her house and connect them to a cast-iron, claw-footed Victorian bath.

In this way, Queenie Bombazine put herself in the lovely position of being able to enjoy hot baths and fresh air at the same time.

Queenie's bath-in-a-field was her favourite possession. Whenever Queenie was in this bath, she was happy. Except today.

Today, even an open-air bath couldn't cheer her up, because that morning she had received a troubling phone call from her accountant, Fiscal Cliff.

Fiscal Cliff had rung with Bad News. His news was on, the one hand, very simple and, on the other, rather complicated and difficult to digest. The news was this: Queenie Bombazine had run out of money. She was skint.

Now Queenie wasn't the kind of person who was particularly interested in money. Not long ago, she had been extremely wealthy, but that hadn't really excited her, and she didn't have much idea where all the money had gone (beyond the occasional plumbing extravagance). But skint, she knew, was a problem. A big problem. Skint meant the gas would be cut off. Skint meant cold baths.

In fact, she definitely remembered having borrowed a large sum of money to buy her large house with its large number of bathing options. Skint, now she thought about it, meant getting kicked out of her home. It meant moving somewhere smaller – somewhere where she might have to use a . . . a . . . and she could hardly allow this word into her brain, it revolted her so much . . . a . . . brace yourselves . . . a . . . are you ready? . . . a . . . shower!

Hideous! Water spraying at you in horrible, jittery-jabby jets! While you stand up! Unspeakable!

Something had to be done. But what?

Queenie had been in the bath for two hours, struggling to think of a plan for how to save her home, when Kevin fell out of the sky and landed on her freshly-washed knee. In a fit of uncharacteristic anger, she tore Kevin into tiny little shreds which she then threw onto the ground. Or tried to, but she couldn't, because the shreds of Kevin stuck to her wet hands.

I'm finished! she thought to herself, scraping half-dissolved Kevin-goo onto the edge of her bath.✱

Queenie, however, wasn't a sulker. She was Queenie Bombazine, circus legend, aerialiste supreme, Mermaid of the Skies (but we'll come to that later). And after her short moment of Kevin-destroying dejection, after her brief little pity-party, a plan pinged into her head. It was the sight of all those other leaves falling from the sky – Kevin's friends✤ – that did it. The way they fluttered to the ground, floating, almost weightless, drifting hither and thither and then

---

✱ Kevin's story ends here. It wasn't a very long story, and it was not a happy one, either. Poor Kevin. He was extremely rude to the branch that looked after him all summer, though, so perhaps he got what he deserved.

✤ Actually, they weren't his friends. Nobody liked Kevin. He was a brat.

hither again reminded her of something.

Queenie reached out and picked up the phone, which she kept on the all-weather cabinet next to her bath, and called her Business Manager, Stage Manager, Tour Manager and Man Manager, Reginald Clench.

'Reginald?' said Queenie. 'I'm calling you with some awful news.'

'Pip pip, Queenie! How are you, what what? I haven't heard from you for ages – not since the last time you ran out of money.'

'What did you say?'

'You heard, duckie.'

'How did you know I'd run out of money?'

'Why else would you call me?'

Reginald was a civilian,♩ and not just an ordinary civilian, but a very civilianny civilian. He was, in fact, a retired army major – strict and disciplined in all matters, punctiliously punctual,

---

♩ This, as you will remember, is what circus folk call non-circus folk. It's not an insult. Not to a civilian, anyway, because civilians don't know any better. To a circus person, calling them a civilian is about as rude as tipping a wellie boot filled with tadpoles into their underpants (i.e. very).

precisely precise and rigorously rigorous. He had served in the British Army for thirty years, until his career was cut short by an unfortunate incident involving a tuba, some goats, a Maharaja's ornamental garden and a runaway steamroller. The details were murky, but, to this day, he still blanched at the sight of a goat. Or a steamroller. Though he did still play the tuba.

Reginald was very much not your usual circus type, but Queenie was strangely fond of him. He was the invisible yet essential element at the heart of all her shows, which starred a large cast of performers, all of whom were eccentric, unpredictable, flighty, flippant and flouncy. The circus needed him in the way a tent needs a tent pole, because without Clench's military discipline, the cast was just thirty people with thirty different ideas, all arguing and bickering and pulling in different directions, the upshot of which would have been thirty very short shows in thirty different places, which is not, by any stretch of the imagination, a circus.

'OK, so you've guessed the awful news,' said Queenie, squeezing the phone in frustration, which caused it to fly out of her soapy hand and plop into the bath.

Queenie often dropped her phone in the bath, so she kept it in a waterproof ziplock bag. She submerged her head and fumbled for the handset in the soapy water, listening for the faint, gurgly sound of Reginald saying, 'Hegluglugllo? Quebubbabubbabeenie? Are you stibubba-bubbabible there?'

It wasn't too long before she fished out the wet, angry-sounding bag.

'Reginald? Hello?'

'It's a very bad line. You sound like you're underwater.'

'Listen – I've made a decision. There's only one thing for it. I'm ready for a comeback. It's time to put on a show.'

The birthday surprise

'THIS IS AN EXTREMELY IMPORTANT birthday,' announced Hannah's father.

Hannah looked down at the kitchen table, which was neatly laid out for her birthday breakfast, with three birthday paper plates, three carefully folded birthday napkins, three balloons and a cake in the shape of a '12'. It was Hannah's father's job to make her birthday cake, and the family tradition was to bake a cake in the shape of the number of Hannah's age.

Hannah's father was kind and decent and loyal, but he was also a very literal man with a very small imagination.

'All birthdays are important,' said Hannah, who wasn't exactly disappointed by the cake, but you couldn't say she was excited, either.

The cake was always the same flavour, carrot cake, which her parents considered to be the healthiest and safest option,△ and though the shape was different each year, the change was never what you would call an exciting surprise.

'But this one is particularly important,' said her dad, 'because the digits of your age form a perfect sequence. That won't happen again until you are twenty-three. And it won't happen with the perfection of starting at the number one unless you live to be one hundred and twenty-three, which at current estimates has a likelihood of less than a quarter of a per cent. So this is almost certainly your only chance.'

'Wow,' said Hannah. This was the only response she could think of.

'And it's important for another reason,' said her mum, whose sombre and serious face at this moment looked even more sombre and serious

---

△ Health and safety, you may remember, were her mother's main concerns. In fact, they were her job.

than usual. Birthday celebration was not Hannah's mother's strong point. 'We've decided that you're old enough to hear some Big News. You were too young to understand what it meant until now. We did some calculations a few years ago, and concluded with as much statistical confidence as one could hope for that 12 is the correct age for us to tell you.'

'Tell me what?'

'Would you like to open your birthday presents first? We've bought you twenty per cent more gifts than the national average, which we think is the right quantity to make you feel special, but not spoilt.'

'I want to hear the news first.'

'You may find it upsetting,' continued her mum, 'so we've taken the precaution of purchasing a different brand of tissues. These ones don't contain the antibacterial agent that may cause irritation to the eyes, and are without the aloe vera that assists nostril healing in the event of a cold. I've decided this is the best kind for the eventuality of weeping.' She handed Hannah a box of tissues. 'If you'd prefer a hanky, that's fine. I'm happy to run a boil wash just this once.'

'I just want you to tell me the news,' said Hannah.

'You may be upset,' warned her mother. 'And it can be very unhealthy to be upset. It's also a leading cause of accidents, so please take extra care in the wake of what I'm about to tell you.'

'I will.'

'Stairs and bathrooms are among the top ten causes of accidental death, so you must take particular care around the home.'

'You've told me that before. Please – I want to know the news.'

'It's this,' said her father. 'You're adopted.'

Hannah's mother plucked out a tissue and put it in Hannah's hand.

'**Wooooooooohoooooooo!**' said Hannah. '**Yipppppeeeeeeeee! Hoooooooodle woooooooooooodle toooooooooooo! I knew it! Wooopidy tooooopidy loooooooooooooo! Iknewit Iknewit Iknewit!**' Hannah wasn't aware of having got up from her chair, but, when she looked down, she saw that her legs were doing a jig and she appeared to be dancing around the kitchen.

She looked across at her parents and saw that they seemed a little dismayed by her reaction, which Hannah – who had impeccable manners – suddenly realised might have been a little rude. She quickly raised the tissue to her eyes and pretended to mop away a tear.

'Oh, gosh!' she said, sitting back down. 'I'm so confused. I don't know what I'm doing. It's just . . .

so upsetting.'

'There, there, dear,' said her mum. 'You just let it all out and have a weep. But not so much that you get dehydrated.'

'I thought you might want to take ownership of this,' said her dad, handing over an important-looking document headed by the words, 'Birth Certificate' in red ink.

'I never knew you got a certificate just for being born,' said Hannah. 'Why didn't you give it to me before?'

'Because of this.'

Hannah's dad was pointing to the words 'Mother's Name', under which was not Hannah's mother's name, but another name entirely: Wendy Bunn.

'Who's Wendy Bunn?' asked Hannah.

'Your birth mother,' said Hannah's mum.

'But that's Granny's surname! That's your maiden name!'

Suddenly, the room filled with an astonishing sound, something like a baying wolf combined with a depressed donkey, a police siren, a Viking war cry and sixty thousand angry mice. Hannah knew the sound well. This was the noise of her mother bursting into tears.

A chair clattered to the floor and Hannah's mum ran out of the room.

'It's an emotional subject,' said her dad, after a long, weird silence. 'Emotions are a valid expression of inner turmoil. You know that, don't you?'

'Why does my birth mother have the same surname as Granny? And why is there a blank where it should say my father's name? Everybody has a father. Who's mine?'

'Would you like to open a present now?' said her father, making the world's most obvious bid to change the subject. 'I'll tell you what it is before you unwrap it if you like, since surprises can put undue pressure on the muscles of the heart.'

'Who's my father?'

'It's a filing cabinet.'

'My father's a filing cabinet?'

'Your present's a filing cabinet. I've decided you're old enough now to keep your own paperwork. It will stand you in good stead for the rest of your life if you start off with a well-alphabetised system. I'll help you set it up.'

'WHO ARE MY REAL PARENTS!?'

A curious choking sound, like a car failing to start, emanated from her father's mouth. 'Oh, my goodness!' he said. 'I'm having an emotion! Oh, gosh. It's quite sickening. I don't think I've had one of these before. I feel dizzy! Is it normal to feel dizzy when you have an emotion? This is horrible! I need an aspirin!'

'Tell me!' snapped Hannah.

'You'll have to ask Granny. I can't speak any more.'

With that, he dashed out of the room, leaving Hannah staring down at her birth certificate and her '12' cake, with only a wrapped filing cabinet for company.

Hannah's birthdays were always disappointing. Every year she told herself not to have high hopes, but every year she ended up disappointed. This year, however, was special. This was deeply weird. She had no idea if she should be whooping or weeping.

Hannah stood up. She didn't unwrap her gift or even taste her cake. There was something far more important to do. She was off to Granny's for an explanation.

At the door, she turned back for the birth certificate, folded it and put it in her pocket. But, as she did so, her eye was caught by one single word scrawled in pencil on the back. This word struck at her heart like a bolt of lightning. Not a full-size bolt of lightning, because that would kill you sure as eggs is eggs,⊙ but a small and jolty one.

The word had a question mark after it, but this didn't make its presence any less shocking, surprising or confusing.

The word was . . . 'SHANK?'

⊙ And eggs really is eggs, most emphatically. You can look it up if you don't believe me. *The Complete History of Eggs* by Daisy Scramble is the place to look. Another option, for a more light-hearted take on the subject, is *Oh Lay, Oh Lay, Olé* by Ringo Kissinger.

THREE
The rampage begins!

ARMITAGE SHANK WAS IN A BAD MOOD.
Obviously. He was always in a bad mood.
He was that kind of person. Bad. And moody.

Two things were bothering him. The first was
that he was still brooding over the disaster of his
last show, when a mysterious, devious and malicious
girl had popped up out of nowhere, tricked his son
Billy, and given all Armitage's carefully stolen
possessions back to their rightful owners.

(Anyone who has read *Circus of Thieves and the*

Raffle of Doom will know that this devious and malicious girl wasn't in fact devious and malicious at all. She was Hannah, who was about as undevious and unmalicious as it is possible to be; but she was clever and resourceful, and when she'd joined forces with Billy, Armitage's plot to rob Hannah's town had fallen apart like a doll in the mouth of a Rottweiler.)

You may remember that Armitage had run away, thinking a sack of his loot was safely stashed in a cunning hiding place. (A bush.) OK, not that cunning. But when he went back, disguised as a travelling fishmonger, to look under his top-secret bush, the loot was gone.

Yes, gone!

He had been diddled, and if there was one thing Armitage didn't like❂ it was being diddled.

He needed that money back. And he needed revenge!♥

❂ There were in fact 7,362 things Armitage didn't like, but there isn't time to go into that here. A few examples: puppies, rainbows, the flute, lifts, turkey, Turkey and trainers with flashing lights in them.

♥ There were only four things Armitage did like: himself, his enormous lorry, gadgets and revenge.

But revenge on who? Because that girl was just a girl and people who are just girls – and civilian girls at that – are in no way powerful or clever enough to diddle the great criminal mastermind, Armitage Shank. Not on your Nellie!

On whose Nellie?

Your Nellie.

Whose?

You! Out there! Holding this book!

But I don't have a Nellie.

That's not important right now.

Who is Nellie, anyway?

I don't know.

Is she an elephant?

Stop arguing. We're wasting time.

Where were we? Oh, yes. Shank was thinking about that meddling, bothersome girl who had robbed him of his robbings. Somebody somewhere must have trained her and sent her to GET HIM!

One of his enemies. The question was, which one?

Armitage wasn't sure.

Some people collect coins, some people collect football stickers, some people collect vintage cars. Armitage collected enemies. So, in circumstances such as this, it was hard for him to figure out who had plotted against him.

On his list of suspects, one name was at the top. 📄

But, before I tell you who that was, I should explain the other thing that was bothering Armitage. It was a jeet he had read that morning.

'A jeet?' I hear you ask. 'What is a jeet?'

Ah, technophobes, the lot of you. All right, I'll explain. Armitage loved gadgets, which was why he stole as many of them as he could. His favourite gadget was his mobile phone, and his favourite thing to do on his phone was to use an

---

📄 Maybe we should add lists to the list of things Armitage liked, because he really was unusually keen on making lists, especially lists of things and people that he didn't like. Once, he made a list of his favourite lists, but that's another story. Look out for *Circus of Thieves and the List of Lists*, soon to be available in all good bookshops, mediocre bookshops, and stinky hovels which happen to have the odd book for sale. 12.3456789% of the royalties will be donated to the Royal Society for the Protection of Numerically Ordered Items (which was founded in 1234 by the fifth Lord Six-Seven of Eight-Nine Hall in Tenby).

antisocial networking service called Jitter. Armitage's phone buzzed and vibrated every time a new message – or jeet – was put up on his Jitter account. Each jeet told him what somebody he knew (or somebody he wanted to know) was either doing, or was about to do, or had just done, or what they thought, or what they thought other people thought, or what they thought of what other people thought about what they thought (are you still with me?). Every time Armitage's phone buzzed, he read the jeet, usually tutted about how boring it was, then put the phone back in his pocket. He did this about seventy-nine times a minute. It was an unhealthy addiction.

But one jeet which he had read that morning came from an old enemy of his. It was this jeet that shifted a particular enemy to the top of his list of suspects.

The jeet was from the legendary, the one and only Queenie Bombazine, and it was quickly rejeeted by thousands of her followers. It was an announcement. An announcement that circus aficionados the world over had been waiting for. Queenie was making a comeback. She was putting on a show.

This, Armitage concluded, was deeply suspicious. She was up to something. All those foolish rejeeters out there might have thought this was just happy news of a circus starlet re-emerging from a period of mysterious hiding, but Armitage had a powerful feeling there was more to Queenie's re-emergence than that. She was out to GET HIM.✿ Or, rather, to GET HIM BACK.

Because Armitage and Queenie had A PAST.

Armitage was determined to get to the BOTTOM of this mystery.☺

✿ Words in capital letters should be shouted aloud.
☺ Did you just shout out 'bottom'? Haha! Tricked you.

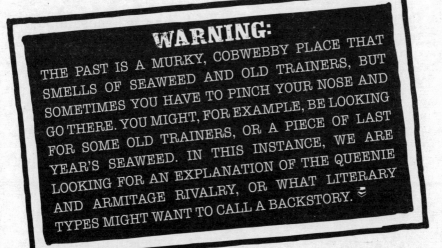

WARNING:

THE PAST IS A MURKY, COBWEBBY PLACE THAT SMELLS OF SEAWEED AND OLD TRAINERS, BUT SOMETIMES YOU HAVE TO PINCH YOUR NOSE AND GO THERE. YOU MIGHT, FOR EXAMPLE, BE LOOKING FOR SOME OLD TRAINERS, OR A PIECE OF LAST YEAR'S SEAWEED. IN THIS INSTANCE, WE ARE LOOKING FOR AN EXPLANATION OF THE QUEENIE AND ARMITAGE RIVALRY, OR WHAT LITERARY TYPES MIGHT WANT TO CALL A BACKSTORY.

Nose-clips on? Here we go, back into those gloomy, doomy, rheumy years known as Armitage's Youth, when he was a young buck on the circus scene, untainted by cynicism, criminality, bad breath or grass stains on his favourite trousers. My, he was a fine specimen. *Phwoooaaargh*, what a hunk! He was just the cat's pyjamas, the kitten's mittens, the feline's beeline. This is not the Armitage we know and loathe, not by any stretch of the meaningless,

---

There's no such thing as a frontstory, by the way. That's just the story. The backstory is what happens before the story begins, then the story is simply the story, and what happens after the story doesn't have a name, because nobody knows what it is, unless another book is written saying what happens after the story, in which case that's a sequel. In fact, this is a sequel, so the last book, which was just a story, is now the backstory to this story, but not the backstory I'm about to tell you about, which happened before the story in the last story, so it might make more sense to call the next bit a backbackstory. Glad we cleared that up,

cat-based metaphor. For not only was he just about the handsomest being ever to be squeezed into a pair of skin-tight trousers, he was also different where it matters. In the heart.

Back then, way back when phones were for

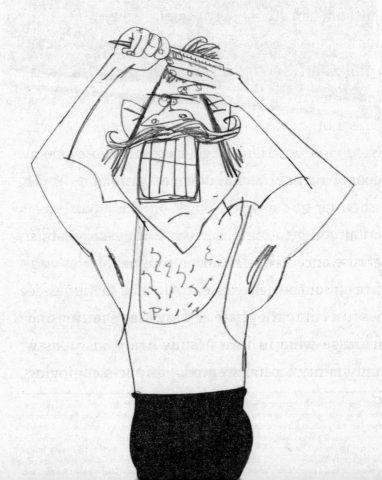

phone calls and computers the size of a garage could just about do the three times table, Armitage had a delicate, fluttery heart, vulnerable to quite overwhelming pangs of love.

Yes, he was still a macho ringmaster with a penchant for flamboyant moustachery, but his muscle-bound, show-offy body was wrapped round a pink, fluffy, vulnerable, palpitating little heart. And, back then, Queenie was in her pomp. (No, that's not a make of car. It just means she was young and beautiful, and was in the process of becoming what she was destined to remain for the rest of her life: a star.)

I'm going to leave out the gloopy, soppy bits, because once a book has been vomited on it is very difficult for the next reader to unstick the pages, so let's just cut to the chase and say that Queenie and Armitage were in love. Handy-holdy, kissy-kissy, fainty-fainty, petal-scented, drippy-song-loving love. Beautiful, it was. Or nauseating. Depending on your viewpoint.

But then, one fateful day, LOVE TURNED TO HATE!

Why?

Well, the trouble started on the day Queenie appeared on the cover of *The Circus Times*. Because even back then, when Armitage was much nicer than he is now, he was prone to bouts of poisonous jealousy.

Until Queenie got on the cover of *The Circus Times*, Armitage had always thought he was the rising star, and his pretty young girlfriend was, well, an adornment. He was the Christmas tree, she was the bauble, so to speak. That's how he thought of it. But, when she became a featured cover artiste, he began to realise that she wasn't just a bauble. She was also the tinsel, the flashing lights, the chocolate coins, the dangly biscuits and

– worst of all – the star on top. Yes, she was *a star*. He was just some foliage.

From that moment on, his love withered. He remained Queenie's boyfriend for a while longer, but he began to criticise, nark, niggle and snipe. She felt sorry for Armitage, not to mention a little guilty that it was her getting all the attention, so for a while she forgave him and politely tolerated the criticising, narking, niggling and sniping. But the day she caught him smearing suntan oil on her trapeze in an attempt to make her fall was the day her patience ran out.

In an instant, her love for him came to an end, like a light switching off, or a train hitting the buffers, or a happy but absent-minded dog accidentally running off the edge of a cliff. In fact, their love didn't just end, it transformed into its opposite.

From that day forth, Armitage and Queenie were sworn enemies.

Queenie left Shank's Impossible Circus to start her own troupe. Not long after that, with audiences dwindling, Shank's Impossible Circus ran into financial difficulties. And, not long after *that*, Armitage turned to crime.

When he committed his first robbery, can you guess who the victim was? Yes, it was Queenie Bombazine. He cleared her out. Picked her clean. Did her over like a kipper.

And you know what she did in return? She ambushed one of his shows, took the brakes off his medium-sized lorry,█ and pushed it into a pond.

A few weeks later, Armitage sneaked into Queenie's costume trailer, took all her costumes, washed them at 60 degrees, and put them all back again, shrunk. *Ha!*

A month or so after this came the itching-powder-in-Armitage's-stage-underpants debacle.

█ This was a few years before he upgraded to an enormous lorry.

When, later that year, Queenie temporarily lost her licence after a clown's exploding cigar exploded ten times more violently than it should have done, setting light to the hair of a granny in the front row, she was in little doubt about who was to blame.

You get the picture. Shank and Bombazine had been rivals and enemies for many, many years. So when Armitage heard that Queenie was making a comeback, and that this was taking place only a short while after his last show had been comprehensively sabotaged, he put these two facts together and came to a conclusion. Two conclusions, in fact. No, three.

CONCLUSION ONE: Queenie Bombazine was to blame for everything.

CONCLUSION TWO: It was time for revenge.

CONCLUSION THREE: Not just ordinary revenge, but a **rampage!**

Armitage leapt out of the shower (did I mention that he was in the shower? Possibly not. It wasn't important until now) and rushed to Narcissus's cage, where he knew he'd find Billy.

'Billy! You'll never guess what I've decided!' he cried.

'Why are you naked?' replied Billy.

'Oh, muffins,' said Armitage. 'I always get forgetful when I decide to go on the rampage.'

'We're going on the rampage?'

'Stay there.'

Armitage rushed back to his caravan, towelled himself dry, and put on his rampaging outfit. When it came to matters of rampage, Armitage had classic tastes. His rampage outfit was a beige safari suit (multi-pocketed, pleated back); safari shorts (beige, with turn-ups); white knee socks (leech-proof); desert boots (beige) and a pith helmet (beige).

He reappeared in Narcissus's cage, where he immediately blended in, what with Narcissus also being beige from head to toe.

'That's . . .'

'Yes! My rampage outfit! This time it's just me and you. Despite your occasional outbreaks of civilian behaviour, you are still heir to the Shank Entertainment Empire, and I've decided that you've reached an age when it's time you learned to rampage. Are you ready?'

'Er . . . I don't know.'

🐪 If you haven't read the last book, Narcissus is a camel. If you have read the last book, but have a poor memory, he is also a camel. If you've read the last book and have a good memory, he's still a camel.

'That wasn't a question, it was a statement.'

'You said, "Are you ready?" That's definitely a question.'

'Stop being cheeky. Do you know what happens to cheeky people?'

'What?'

'I said, DO YOU KNOW WHAT HAPPENS TO CHEEKY PEOPLE?'

'Why are you shouting?'

'Because you said "what?"'

'I meant "what?" as in "what happens to cheeky people?"'

'I don't know. What does happen to cheeky people?'

'I don't know,' replied Billy. 'You asked me.'

'Did I?'

'Yes.'

'Look, we're getting sidetracked,' said Armitage, tightening the chinstrap on his pith helmet. 'I'm telling you you're old enough for a rampage. You *are* ready. Now go and get ready.'

'You said I was already ready.'

'Ready as in old enough. Now go and get ready as in *changed*.'

'Into what?'

'Something more rampagey. Something hard-wearing, quick-drying and suited to sudden changes in climate.'

'Like what?'

'I don't know. Jeans and a T-shirt or something.'

'What kind of a rampage are we going on?'

'The best kind. A thieving rampage and a revenge rampage, rolled into one. I have a plan so devastatingly, demonically, deviously dastardly that if I told you what it was, it would probably melt your eardrums. We're going to be rich. Rich, I say, rich. RICH! Hahahahahahahahahaaaaaa!'

'I don't get the joke.'

'What joke?'

'Why are you laughing?'

'I wasn't laughing, I was cackling. They're very different. Now go and get changed.'

Billy gave Narcissus a last handful of pellets and a quick slurp of taramasalata, then went to change his clothes. He was an obedient boy. Obedient, that is, when he wasn't trying to get his stepfather caught by the police and locked up in jail for the rest of his life, which, let's face it, doesn't usually fall into the bracket of obedience.

Part of him dreaded the idea of going off with his stepfather,♟ just the two of them, without the rest of the circus troupe to dilute Armitage's attentions. And why was Billy so reluctant to spend some quality time with his father-out-law? Well, mainly because Armitage was a revolting slug of a human being without any shred of decency, courtesy, morality, honesty, kindness, humour or

---

♟ Or perhaps that should be circus-father. Or stolen-from-your-real-father-father. There isn't really a suitable term for Armitage's relationship to Billy. Perhaps father-out-law does the best job. If you're confused, read the last book. If, after that, you're still confused, read it again. Then, if you're still confused, give up and go to bed.

humility. That more or less sums up the downside. But, on the other hand, Billy's curiosity had been pricked by that word *rampage*. He didn't quite know what Armitage meant, but it sounded interesting. It sounded like an adventure.

Just as Billy was entering his caravan, pondering whether or not something exciting was about to happen on the trip that lay ahead, something exciting happened right there and then, in front of him.

A man appeared. (OK, it doesn't sound that exciting, but bear with me.)

A man appeared out of the sky.

'Implausible!' you cry. 'Men don't appear out of skies.'

All right, all right. A man *seemed* to appear out of the sky, when in fact he had jumped down from the roof of Billy's caravan.

This was no ordinary man, either. He was dressed in black and white stripes, with a chain around his ankle, and the words **PROPERTY OF HM PRISON GRIMWOOD SCRUBS: IF YOU SEE ME WALKING AROUND OR JUMPING OFF THE ROOF OF CARAVANS, BEWARE BECAUSE I AM AN ESCAPED CONVICT** written on his back.

Billy, who was a perceptive chap, concluded that this was an escaped convict. If he'd been a screamy kind of person, it's about now that Billy would have let rip with a right proper belter.

'I've been waiting for you,' said the escaped convict.

If Billy had been the bedwetting sort, it's at roughly this moment that he would have broken with nocturnal tradition and weed in his trousers.

'I'm a friend of your father,' said the man. 'He was jailed for a crime he didn't commit, and so was I. We've shared a cell for the last five years, keeping each other going by playing games of chess with carved toenail clippings. Your dad's rubbish at chess, and that's what kept me sane. He never beat me once. And he asked me to give you this!'

From his pocket, the man pulled out a letter, on which were written two words that cured Billy instantly of his fear and made his heart dance a very small tango of delight. His name. Not Billy Shank, but a name he hadn't heard for a long, long time. His real name. Billy Espadrille.

'Who are you?' said Billy.

'I'm Magwitch Intertextuality McDickens. Your father talked about you all the time, except for when he was swearing about losing another game of chess. He loves you very, very, very much. If he wasn't locked up, he would have come and got you ages ago. Read the letter. Though it might be a bit boring now, because I've told you most of what's in it. Sorry. I have to go. Oh, wait, I forgot the best bit!'

'What's that?'

'They're letting your dad out this week! He's going to come and get you.'

'Really!? But how will he find me?' Billy was trembling with excitement.

'Same way I did.'

'And how was that?'

'I hid on top of your caravan,' replied the convict, looking surprised that Billy had already forgotten.

'But how did you find my caravan?'

'Guesswork. Bye.'

Then Magwitch Intertextuality McDickens was gone, leaving behind only the faint odour of unwashed feet and boiled cabbage.

Billy hurried into his caravan and read the letter. It wasn't even slightly boring, though it did say exactly what Magwitch Intertextuality McDickens had already told him, except with dodgy spelling and totally b'onk-er:s p,un?ctu/!!ation;. Ernesto Espadrille♧♧ was almost as bad at punctuation as he was good at juggling.

His father was coming to rescue him! This was the best news ever! Even better news than the day when a TV newsreader went loopy and announced that the government had decided to disband the army and spend all the money on free chocolate. Yes, news just didn't get any better than this. Not ever.

Except that Billy was about to set off on the rampage. So, even if Ernesto did guess the location of the caravan, Billy wouldn't be there.

And how would his father know where to look? Guesswork didn't sound like a promising strategy, especially given that the whole point of Shank's Impossible Circus was that nobody ever knew where they were, because there were so many people out to get them, not least every law-enforcement official in the entire country.

♧♧ That's Billy's father. His real father. Keep up.

So how *had* Magwitch McDickens found him?

And how had he escaped?

And why was he a convict?

And there's no way you can play toenail clipping chess every day for five years without even winning once, surely.

Mystery upon mystery, baked into mystery cake, iced with mystery icing, decorated with mystery sweets and mystery candles, served on a mystery plate in a mystery room to mystery people in mystery masks blowing mystery party tooters and . . . can I stop with this yet?

FOUR

Granny becomes a double granny

'GRANNY, GRANNY, GRANNY!' yelled Hannah. 'I've just been told the weirdest thing ever, but it doesn't make any sense! I need you to explain.'

It was no use. Hannah was too impatient. She would have to go round to Granny's house before she started yelling for explanations.

She ran there as fast as she could.

'Granny, Granny, Granny!' yelled Hannah. 'I've just been told the weirdest thing ever, but it doesn't make any sense! I need you to explain.'

No, impatience was still getting the better of her. She had to ring the doorbell first.

She rang the doorbell.

Granny opened the door.

'Granny, Granny, Granny!' yelled Hannah. 'I've just been told the weirdest thing ever, but it doesn't make any sense! I need you to explain.'

'Hang on a second, dear, I haven't got my hearing aid in yet. Have a gobstopper.'

Hannah took the gobstopper and a seat in the living room. Granny went upstairs (which took a while), looked for her hearing aid (which took another while), put it in (one while more), then came downstairs again (which was really fast, because she slid down the banister). She sat opposite Hannah, in a chair so densely covered in purple embroidered roses that it made your eyes hurt to look at it.

'Now, dear. What's the trouble?' she asked.

'Grnnng, Grnnng, Grnnng!' yelled Hannah. 'I'nk jush bing yold hte heerdnest ning nivr, buu is yonts's makl ang shints! H neee woo ta hxplxn.'

'Pardon?'

Granny fiddled anxiously with her hearing aid.

Hannah took out the gobstopper.

'Granny, Granny, Granny!' she yelled, slightly hoarse now, and with rather less enthusiasm than when she'd started. 'I've just been told the weirdest thing ever, but it doesn't make any sense! I need you to explain.'

'It's your birthday, isn't it?' replied Granny. 'You're twelve now, aren't you?'

'Yes, Granny.'

'So your parents have told you the Big Secret?'

'Yes! But I don't understand!'

'Well, it's a rather long story. Would you like a cup of tea first?'

'No thanks.'

'Juice?'

'No thanks.'

'Banana?'

'Please, Granny. Just tell me the story.'

'OK, dear. Well, it all goes back a long, long way. We have to go right back to the day you were born. No, we have to go back to the day your mother was born. Or, rather, your mothers.'

'Mothers?'

'Yes, mothers. You see your mother – your current mother – is a twin. You have an aunt you've never met. Except she isn't your aunt. She's your mother. Your other mother. Your birth mother.'

'I thought you said you were going to explain. This is just even more confusing.'

'Put the gobstopper back in, dear, and let me tell you the whole thing. Your mother isn't my only daughter. I had twins. Wendy and Wanda. They weren't identical twins, and they weren't even non-identical twins. They were opposite-in-every-way-you-can-imagine twins. Wanda, your mother – your current mother – is as you know a very cautious, careful and safety-conscious person. She didn't walk until she was two, because she thought crawling was safer. Wendy, your other mother – your birth mother – walked at six months, fell over all the time, visited A&E every few weeks, and liked nothing better than launching herself down a staircase just to see what would happen.'

'Hak ma mrrrrbit?'

'Pardon?'

Hannah took out the gobstopper.

'That's my mother? My real mother?'

'It is. She was a wild one from the start. I always worried about her – always knew she'd get herself into trouble – and she did. She was only a teenager when she ran away to the circus. Can't say I was surprised. And when she told me she'd discovered a talent for the trapeze, and had learned that she was never happier than when spinning through the air of a Big Top, that was hardly a shock, either. But I was surprised when she came back for a visit and told me that she was in love, and that she had a problem, because she couldn't tell who she was in love with.'

'What?'

'There were two men from two rival circuses, and they'd both told her they loved her. Wendy knew she was in love, because she felt fluttery and

flighty and flouncy and flushed, but she couldn't
tell which man she was in love with. She said they
were both in the car outside, and asked me if I
could take a look at them and give her my advice.
Now this was very unusual for Wendy, because she
was not the kind of girl who ever asked my advice
about anything, but I was happy to help, so I said
she should bring them in, and I'd take a look, and
set them the Cupcake Test.'

Granny's stories were always like this. Stories
within stories within stories, like Russian dolls.
Once she'd started telling you something, before
she got to the end, she'd always divert into telling
you something else about somebody else. Hannah
knew better than to fight it. If you waited long
enough, Granny usually worked her way back to
the starting point.

'The Cupcake Test?' asked Hannah, with a
mixture of curiosity and impatience.

'Yes. The Cupcake Test. You sit them both down, and hand the boyfriend a plate, on which are two cupcakes. A big one and a small one. If he takes the small one, he shows that he's kind and considerate, and he passes. If he takes the big one, he's clearly selfish and arrogant and rude, and he fails. It tells you everything you need to know about how this person is going to treat your precious daughter.'

'So what happened?'

'Well, Wendy brought in these two young men, and I have to say they were both extremely handsome. Not that looks are the most important thing, but golly they really were quite delectable . . .'

'Granny?'

'What?'

'You've drifted off.'

'Sorry. Yes. So she brought in these two young chaps, and I brought out a plate with three cupcakes on it, two big and one small. And I handed the plate

to the first one – the one with a moustache – and you know what he did?'

'What?'

'He took all three! Gobbled them down and didn't even say thank you. I knew straight away that he was a wrong'un. Despicable! And I told her so! But did she listen? Did she?'

'Did she?'

'I don't know. The other chap was lovely. A proper gentleman. I handed him a refilled plate and he gave both cupcakes to Wendy, then stood up and poured everyone tea and handed it round without even being asked. And you should have seen his muscles! Not that muscles are important, but when he held the teapot his forearms rippled and bulged and . . . Anyway, I told Wendy what I thought, but just as Wendy was not the kind of girl to ask for advice, she was also not the kind of girl to listen to advice when it was given. I knew she was falling deeper in love after that, because one of the symptoms of love is that you stop phoning your mother. I didn't hear from her for a while, except for a postcard from Moscow saying that she wanted me to post her a pair of gloves, and that she was married, and that she'd tell me all about it as soon as she got home.'

'And?'

'Well, the circus was on a world tour, and a few months after that I got a card from Mexico City asking me to post her some tea bags, and saying that she was pregnant, and that it was the most exciting thing ever, and she'd tell me all about it as soon as she got home.'

'And?'

'I heard nothing for a year or so, then one day, out of the blue, the doorbell rang.'

'It was her?'

'No. It was a camel. Holding a basket in its mouth. And in the basket was a postcard from Johannesburg saying that the circus world tour was the trip of a lifetime, but that travelling conditions in Africa were not suitable for a young baby. Next to the postcard, in the basket, was a baby. You. The card said she'd be back soon to take care of you. But we heard nothing for two more years, until finally, out of the blue, the doorbell rang.'

'And this time it was her?'

'No. It was the camel again, with a basket holding a black envelope and a small parcel wrapped in brown paper. The envelope contained nothing except a newspaper cutting from the *Auckland Examiner*, describing a trapeze accident that had led to the tragic death of an aerial artiste.'

'My mother's dead?'

'Yes, Hannah, I'm sorry. Your birth mother is dead. But your aunt raised you, and she put her heart and soul into it, and even though you and she may not see eye to eye, she's been as good a mother to you as anyone could want.'

'So my mother's not my mother, but you're still my granny?'

'I'm your double granny, because I'm the mother of both your mothers. And what could be better than that?'

'If my real mum was alive, *that* would be better,' said Hannah, only just holding back a surge of sobs.

'I'm so sorry, dear,' said Granny. 'We all tried our best for you.'

'I know you did,' replied Hannah, who at this moment felt as if her heart was being used as a trampoline. 'And my father never came back for me?'

'I'm afraid not.'

'You never saw him again?'

'I'm not sure.'

'You're not sure?'

'Well, like I said, your father could be either of those two chaps, but the one I didn't like, the one with the moustache, I think we both may have come across him this summer. And I think he might be an even worse fellow than my Cupcake Test told me.'

'Not . . . ?'

'Yes!'

'Not . . . ?'

'YES!'

'Not . . . ?'

'OH, YES! Armitage Shank. That was him. I recognised him instantly.'

'And the other one? The nice one? Who was he?'

'I don't know.'

'What was his name?'

'I can't remember. But he really did have lovely muscles. And he was so polite. It must have been him. I'm sure your father's that one.'

'You're sure?'

'I think I'm sure. But your mother was a headstrong girl. Very unpredictable. I'm so sorry about all this, Hannah. It really is quite confusing, isn't it?'

Hannah nodded, and a tingle at the end of her nose alerted her to the fact that her sobs could be held in no longer.

Granny fetched a box of tissues, rubbed Hannah's back, kissed her seven times on the forehead, then began to rummage in a high cupboard. She returned with a small parcel wrapped in brown paper.

'This is the parcel?' sniffled Hannah.

Granny nodded and opened it on the coffee table. Inside was layer upon layer of pink crêpe paper. Under the crêpe paper was a green rubber catsuit with a yellow lightning bolt streaking across the chest and down one leg.

'This is all we got back from the circus. It's her trapeze outfit.'

Hannah lifted up the costume and stared. She had never seen anything so beautiful. She raised it to her wet, tingly nose and sniffed. An aroma of absolute perfect and exquisite rightness drifted into her. She inhaled and inhaled, sucking her mother's scent into her. Then Hannah saw the sequinned words embroidered on the back: 'Esmeralda Espadrille'.

'WHHHAAAAAAT!?' shrieked Hannah. 'Esmeralda Espadrille! That's my mother?'

'Yes. That was her stage name. She could do a back somersault from trapeze to trapeze with a double pike, triple flip-flop and . . .'

'. . . quadruple wing-ding. I know.'

'How do you know?'

'I met her son. Billy. It was him and me who took the enormous lorry and stole back Armitage's loot.'

'His lute? I didn't know he played the lute.'

'No, the stuff that he'd stolen. His *loot*.'

'*That was Wendy's son?*'

'It was Esmeralda Espadrille's son. And if

they're the same person . . .'

'THEY ARE! I knew it!' said Granny. 'I mean, I didn't know it. But I should have. The minute I saw the way that boy handled a camel I knew he was . . . was . . .'

'Special?' offered Hannah.

'Yes. Special like your mother was special. Special like you're special. And, now I think of it, I recognise that camel – strong profile, movie-star eyelashes and a good set of long green teeth – and I'm sure that's the camel who delivered you.'

Hannah's heart was now beginning to feel like a trampoline and a trapeze and a drum kit, all at once. This had been a deeply strange day. She'd lost a mother and father, then found another mother only to discover that she was dead, found two potential new fathers, and now it dawned on her that she might have gained a . . . no, she couldn't let herself think it until she knew for sure.

'So, if Esmeralda Espadrille is my mother, and she's also Billy's mother, does that mean Billy's my brother?' she asked.

'I suppose it does. Or your half-brother at least. That all depends on who your father is and who Billy's father is.'

'The other man who came round that day – the Cupcake Test day – was he called Ernesto?'

'I think he might have been. It's definitely a name with that kind of sound, because I remember telling myself not to call him Tesco by accident. Or maybe he was called Clive. I think it was one or the other.'

'We have to find Billy and get the truth! He's my brother!'

'He's my grandson!'

'So let's go!' said Hannah, leaping up.

'Let's go!' replied Granny, leaping up, too.

'But where?' said Hannah, sitting down. 'How

are we going to find them? Shank's Impossible Circus is on the run. In hiding. And nobody knows where Ernesto is, either. Do they?'

❦ 'Oi!' I hear you shout. Unfortunately, I don't respond to rudeness.

❦ 'Excuse me, sir?' I hear you ask. Too much. Sycophantic.

❦ 'Ahem,' you cough. 'I have a question.' That's more like it. 'At the end of the last book it seemed like Hannah was going to follow Narcissus's footprints and find Billy straight away. What about that? Eh?' OK. Good point. Very clever. Very astute. Very alert. You see . . . the thing is . . . er . . . what happened was . . . um . . . the fact is . . . it rained that night. Really hard. And washed away the footprints. OK? Satisfied? Smartypants.

The Oh, Wow!

YOU **MAY HAVE READ ABOUT THIS** in the
newspapers already, but just in case it passed
you by, now is probably a good time to tell you
about a strange event of national importance
that happened several years ago. It was a hot
summer's day, somewhere towards the tail end
of the last century, and Parliament was filled
with dozy, sweaty MPs, busy debating and dozing
and sweating. The Prime Minister himself felt
particularly thirsty and hot, which in his case

combined with a sudden overpowering urge to drink something blue. He sent out one of his minions for a Slush Puppy, which he foolishly drank in one go, giving him a huge brainfreeze.

In the grip of this brainfreeze, he suddenly stood up and yelled, 'Let's build a massive tent in the middle of nowhere and fill it with interesting stuff! It'll be incredible! Trust me on this!'

Everyone there was too hot and dozy to object, but by the time the tent was eventually built the brainfreeze had worn off, and the Prime Minister couldn't remember what interesting things he'd had in mind to put inside it. The upshot was a massive pointless tent in the middle of nowhere, which sat there for a few years, as a monument to _____,✎ until an international consortium of property developers called Yeravinalarf Incorporated bought the site at a knock-down price and turned it into an entertainment venue

---

✎ You can fill in the blank yourself. There are many options. For example: vanity, waste, political insanity, the delusions of power, brainfreezes, tents.

called the Oh, Wow! Centre.

Now Queenie Bombazine happened to be an old acquaintance of the Oh, Wow! Centre's Operations Manager, a man called Kelvin Pype, who by a curious coincidence had once been Queenie Bombazine's second-favourite plumber. She called him up, reminisced for a while about a blocked U-bend, back in the good old days when U-bends were U-bends and days were good and old, then she told him about her plan for a comeback show. She wanted to book the Oh, Wow! Centre for two nights.

'Oh, wow!' replied Pype, who was something of a circus aficionado, and was fully aware of the legendary status of La Bombazine. He immediately agreed, on condition that she'd give him a seat in the front row for every performance and autograph his bottom. (He was a BIG fan.) Queenie Bombazine, who had seen it all before (not his bottom – I simply mean she had come across all kinds of eccentric behaviour), agreed, with a weary sigh. Fans, these days, really were getting weirder. After one of her last performances, she'd been asked to sign a full-size, home-made, papier-mâché hippopotamus. There was simply no way of explaining what people wanted from her.

It was hard, indeed, being a celebrity. Harder than it used to be, back in the good old days when U-bends were U-bends and celebrities were left alone. In fact, that was one of the reasons why she had retired, the other one being that trapeze careers have a habit of coming to a sticky end (literally). Queenie didn't believe in safety nets, but she also didn't believe in plummeting to her doom for the entertainment of strangers, so, when the day came that she felt the strength in her arms beginning to weaken, she decided to call it quits before she came a cropper. But that, of course, was before she came a cropper in a quite different way, by plummeting to her doom from cosy, multiple-bathroomed richness to chilly, horrid skintness.

The Oh, Wow! deal was arranged by phone, from Queenie's bath. Barely had she hung up than she heard the sound of Reginald Clench's motorbike puttering up her driveway. Queenie had a long driveway. That's how rich she was. Or had been, when she bought the house. 'Pip pip,' tootled Clench as he parked up and strode across the field to Queenie's bath. His Labrador, Rudolph, leapt out of the sidecar and marched alongside, in step with his owner.

The dog marched?

Yes.

Marched?

Stop arguing. Rudolph the dog marched. Clench was a military man and he'd trained Rudolph as he would have trained any young recruit. If you've never seen a dog march – and you probably haven't

– then you'll just have to imagine it. It's more or less the same as a normal soldier's march, except with more legs.

'Hello, Reginald,' said Queenie. 'I've booked us the Oh, Wow! Centre for two nights.'

'That's top-hole!' said Reginald, who was delighted to have his enforced retirement coming to an end. He didn't even like weekends, so for him retirement was a dismal nightmare of relentless tedium, which he could only fill by carrying a toolbox with him wherever he went and performing almost constant DIY. During some of his lowest moments, he'd been known to break things just so he could fix them again.

'How are we doing for infantry . . . I mean, performers?' he asked.

'I was just going to make a few calls.'

'Good idea. You chat 'em up, talk the talk, then pass 'em over and I'll take care of the money. Let's get weaving. No time like the present. Rolling stone and all that, what what?'

They got weaving. Queenie Bombazine made her calls, though it wasn't so easy to track everyone down, since her old troupe was so loyal to Queenie that when she'd retired most of them had taken the decision to bow out of circusry altogether rather than work for someone else.

Her first call was to Jemima Steam, the nautical

fire-eater. It turned out she was now working as a pearl diver in the Maldives, but the minute she heard about the Oh, Wow! Centre revival, she vowed to get on the next flight home and be there in time for the show.

Next up was Zygmond Tszyx, the trampolining bubble wizard, who was now the Transport Minister of Hungary. But Budapest would just have to remain gridlocked, because Zygmond Tszyx was in, and he was bringing along his son, Zygmond Tszyvn.

Then there was Cissy Noodles and her swimming poodles. Cissy now ran Alaska's most popular chain of Mongolian Barbecue restaurants, but Alaska was going to be just that little bit hungrier from now on, because, yes, Noodles and her oodles of poodles were going home.

The Aquabats of Arabia were still together, but now working as car mechanics in Wigan. They signed up, too, quicker than you can say spark plug.

Bunny Weasel and her synchronised otters had fallen on hard times. She was now a prison officer in Ushuaia, which is the southernmost prison in the world, at the very bottom of Argentina. She'd been locked up there for pickpocketing, but, following a bet with a drunken prison guard about whether she could teach a cockroach to do a dance routine (which she won (it was a foxtrot)), she'd switched places with the guard, who was now serving out the rest of her sentence.

But there was no way of knowing what would happen to that foolish prison guard now, because Bunny was on her way to the Oh, Wow!

Ruggles Pynchon, the magician-recluse, was the hardest to find. Eventually, via his publisher,♠ Queenie tracked down a top-secret phone number and called

---

♠ He had written a book of card tricks which literally nobody understood, but which all the newspapers said was a masterpiece, because nobody wanted to be the first to admit they couldn't understand it.

him. At the moment he picked up, he was inside an air-conditioning shaft in the Kremlin,♔ where he'd been working for several months as a spy. Under the code name The Kremlin Gremlin, he'd been sneaking around hiding biros, moving car keys, unmatching socks in the president's sock drawer, and misaligning the perforations on toilet rolls. It was all very top secret – a mission known only to those in MI6 with super-ultra-mega-whopper security clearance level 17. But, when he got the call from Queenie, that was it. Bye-bye civil service pension. Ruggles was off. And Queenie Bombazine's Ecstatic Aquatic Splashtastic Circus of the Century was on!

Three and a half seconds after the tickets went on sale, every single one was sold. Even the seats at the very back, from where you could only see the stage through a telescope.

♔ The Kremlin is Russia's HQ – kind of like Parliament, 10 Downing Street and Buckingham Palace all rolled up together, hidden behind a massive wall, with a few domes plonked on top and Very Serious Men outside practising silly walks.

SIX

The mountain tandem

GRANNY LED HANNAH down to her basement. It was a dark, cobwebby place that smelt of seaweed and old trainers, which is slightly confusing, since on this occasion time was behaving properly and heading politely forward in an orderly way as it was taught to do in school. Although, having said that, going down into Granny's basement was a bit like going into the past, since it was stacked to the ceiling with very old things from very long ago, all of which belonged in either a museum or the bin. 🏛

🏛 I said that thing about a museum just to be polite. Actually, it all belonged in the bin. This is just between us, OK?

In among the mounds of dusty artefacts from Granny's past, one object stood out. It stood out because it was sparkling clean, glistening with up-to-dateness.

It was a bike. No ordinary bike, but a tandem. And no ordinary tandem, either, but what you would have to call a mountain tandem. It had massive chunky tyres, wide chunky mudguards, chunky pedals, chunky handlebars, a chunky bell, and chunks of chunks bolted onto the chunky frame just for the sheer chunkiness of it. This bike was chunky.

'I customised it myself,' said Granny. 'Brought it up to date for our trip.'

'But how did you know we were going on a trip?'

'Because I knew you were going to be told the truth about your past on your twelfth birthday, and I know you're not the kind of girl to take something like that lying down. You're not even the kind of girl to take it standing up. You're the kind of girl to go straight round to her granny's house demanding to know the truth and, if what she tells you doesn't stack up, insisting on setting off on a trip to find out what needs to be found out. That's the kind of girl you are. And it's the kind of girl your mother was, too. So I got this bike ready as your birthday present. It used to be Wendy and Wanda's.'

'It's fantastic!' said Hannah. 'I love it! Thank you!'

'Happy Birthday my love.'

They hugged a big size twelve birthday hug, but not for long. There wasn't time.

'So, lets go!' said Hannah

'Let's go!'

Hannah and Granny heaved the bike up from the basement. They were just about to climb on when an important question occurred to Hannah.

'Wait!' she said. 'Where are we actually going?'

'To find your father. To find Billy.'

'I know that, but *where*? We don't know who my father is and we don't know where Billy is.'

'Aaah,' said Granny, 'we don't know where they are now, but I'm pretty sure where they will be this weekend.'

'How could you possibly know that?'

'I've had a text message from an old friend of mine. She's coming out of retirement. She's putting on a comeback show. And, when *she* puts on a show, *everyone* who has *anything* to do with *any* circus *anywhere* goes along to watch.'

This idea excited Granny so much that she trembled and quivered and gesticulated and knocked the bike over, but the bike was so chunky it just laughed and said, 'Ha! I didn't even feel that! Not a thing!'

'Besides,' said Granny, 'this friend of mine has some history with your father. Or, rather, with one of your fathers. Or one of the people who might be your father.'

'You're being very confusing,' said Hannah, as she picked up the bike.

'My friend is called Queenie Bombazine and Armitage Shank detests her. She's his oldest enemy. So I'm sure he'll be at her comeback show, trying to get revenge of some sort. I just know it. Sure as eggs is eggs.' ⊛

'And do you think Billy will be with him?'

'Definitely.'

'Oh, Wow!'

'How did you know?'

'Know what?'

'Where the show is going to be.'

'I don't know,' said Hannah, giving Granny an I-love-you-but-you're-bonkers look.

'But you just said it!'

'Said what?'

⊛ See the books mentioned earlier if you still require proof of the egginess of eggs. Alternatively, make an egg sandwich, leave it in your sock drawer for a week, then shove your face in and take a good whiff. This is one of the eggiest proofs of egginess that can be conducted safely outside a laboratory. Do not attempt this if you are prone to fainting or share a bedroom.

'The Oh, Wow! That's where they'll be.'

'Granny, I think you might be having a sugar crash. You're just talking complete gibberish.'

'The Oh, Wow! Centre. The massive, pointless tent in the middle of nowhere! That's where Queenie's putting on her circus! I've got us tickets already.'

'Oh, great!'

'Oh, Wow!'

'OK.'

'OK! So let's go!'

'Let's go.'

And off they went, heading directly for the middle of nowhere, the bike laughing again as they set off, saying, 'Two of you? Is that all? I could take three! I could take five! I could take sixty-eight! Feel my chunks! Go on, feel my chunks!'

SEVEN

The rampage begins!

AT EXACTLY THE SAME MOMENT, Armitage and Billy were also setting off. Yes, exactly the same moment. Spooky, isn't it, when connected things happen in different places at the same time? Yes, the same time! I'm scaring myself now. I'm going to have to hide under the sofa for a bit and eat a biscuit, until I've calmed down.

They travelled all of three centimetres before encountering their first problem. An angry head, sticking out of the window of a caravan, yelled in

---

⊙ Middle-class parents reading this aloud have my formal permission to replace the word 'biscuit' with the words 'oatcake and slices of organic apple'.

an angry voice: 'Oi! Where do you think you're going? I know that outfit! You're on the rampage! What's going on?'

It was Frank, the clown. Or maybe it was Hank, the other clown.

'Are you leaving us behind?' yelled another angry voice, from out of the same window.

This was Hank. Or maybe Frank.

'Ow! My neck!' yelled Hank/Frank.

'What's wrong with your neck?' yelled Frank/Hank.

'I had this window first.'

'Well, I had it second.'

'It's not big enough for two!'

'Yes it is!'

'No it isn't!'

'Yes it is! Why are you so selfish?'

'Why are *you* so selfish?'

'Why are *you* so selfish?'

'Why can't you use the other window?'

'Why can't *you* use the other window?'

'Hong heuuurrghhhhh!' yelled someone else, now sticking his head out of the window of another caravan. This was Maurice: professional acrobat, professional Frenchman. 'What's going on! I'm in ze meedle of a massage! Can't an 'umble genius of strrrength and dexterity 'ave a moment's peace?'

'Billy and Armitage are going on the rampage!' yelled Hank and Frank together. 'Without us!'

'There's no need to be suspicious,' said Armitage. 'It's just a little father and son bonding trip.'

'Hah!' said Fingers O'Boyle, the magician who was so light-fingered his fingers sometimes almost floated away. He was at that moment returning from his morning swim, dressed in a strikingly simple outfit, which seemed to consist of one leaf.❋ 'When a criminal tells you not to be suspicious, it's time to be very suspicious. What are you up to, Shank?'

'Up to?' said Armitage, in his most innocent voice (which was in fact not very innocent at all). 'I simply think it's time to teach the boy some rudiments of rampage technique. That's all. Just a spot of harmless practice.'

'I don't trust you,' said Fingers.

'*I* don't trust you,' said Maurice.

'*I* don't trust you,' said Hank (or maybe it was Frank).

'*I* don't trust you,' said Frank (or maybe it was Hank).

❋ This leaf, by a strange coincidence, was Kevin's cousin, and it was not happy to end up as a swimming costume. Kevin was from a very unlucky family.

'*I* don't trust anyone,' said Irrrrrena, Maurice's assistant, peeping 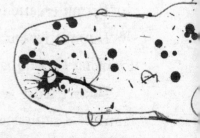 out of the front door of her caravan.

'Who doesn't trust who?' said Jesse, emerging from underneath the enormous lorry, smeared in oil. Jesse was the only person, apart from Armitage, who was allowed to touch the enormous lorry. Armitage would have done the repairs himself, except that he didn't know how, and couldn't bear the idea of getting his clothes dirty. Jesse was also the world's most reluctant human cannonball.

'Of course you don't trust me,' said Armitage. 'Only a fool would trust me. I'm a professional cheat and a sneak and a liar and a thief. What kind of a fool would trust *me*?'

'I would,' said Jesse.

☉☉ The second 'p' is very important in this word. Without it, a very different scene is conjured up.

'Thank you, Jesse. Excellent. Now keep up the good work, everyone. I'm just taking Billy on a short and entirely harmless rampage practice, and we'll be back before you know it. Bye!'

And off they went.

✳

'So this is it?' said Billy, after a mile or so. 'This is a rampage?'

'Mmm,' replied Armitage, whose entire attention was focused on his satnav. 'We're going to go down the B2893 for 2.1 miles, then down the A234 for 7.6 miles,[zzz] onto the A18 for 32.4 miles, then we'll turn onto the M1½ for 97 miles before turning onto the A16 for 7.1 miles, then the B8293 for 2.1 miles, and the B764 and the B983, then onto local roads which will lead us to our destination.'

'That's a rampage, is it?'

'Yes.'

'A real rampage or a practice rampage?'

[zzz] Most books have a boring bit somewhere that you can skip. Teachers never admit to this, but it's true. This paragraph is a good example of a Very Boring Bit. I recommend that you jump immediately to the next paragraph, because what remains of this one is pure, undiluted, top-of-the-range tedium.

'A real one, of course! I just had to say something to put those idiots off the scent.'

'I thought rampages were supposed to be . . . I don't know . . . a bit wilder than this.'

'No,' said Armitage. 'At least, not yet! **HahahahahahaHAHAHAHAHAhahahaha!**'

'I don't get it.'

'Get what?'

'Why are you laughing?'

'Oh, for goodness sake Billy. You have to learn the difference between a laugh and a cackle. You're never going to get very far in the criminal underworld if you can't even cackle. Listen. Copy me. **HahahahahaHAHAHAHAhahahaha!**'

'Hahahhahahhahahaha!'

'No, **HahahahahaHAHAHAHAhahahaha!**'

'HahahahahHAHAhahahaha!'

'Better. Try again. **Hahahahahahahahaha HAHAHAHAHAhahahahahahaha!**'

'HahahahahahahaHAHAHAHAHAHAhahahaha!'

'Nearly. **HahahahahahahahaHAHAHAHA HAHAHAHAHAHAhahahhahahahahaha!**'

'**HAHAHAHAHAHAHAHA HAHAHAHAHAHAHAHAHA HAHAHAHAHAHAHAHA!**'

'Too much,' said Armitage, sternly. 'Much too much. We can have another practice tomorrow.'

'In forty metres, turn right,' said the satnav, which was attached to the handlebars of Armitage's scooter.

Did I not mention the scooter? How silly of me.

Even though it wounded Armitage to the core to be parted for even a day from his beloved lorry, he had decided that for this particular rampage a less enormous mode of transport would be needed. To carry out his dastardly plan, it was important that he and Billy didn't draw attention to themselves, so enormousness was out. As a result,

Armitage was on a scooter and Billy was riding Narcissus.

Only as they were turning onto the M1½, with a busload of children staring and pointing at them, did it occur to Armitage that these modes of transport weren't exactly helping them blend into the background, either.

'Hmm,' he said. 'We're going to have to do something about that camel. He's too circussy. People are noticing us.'

Narcissus, who even for a camel was quick to take offence, gargled up a tennis-ball-sized dollop of camel goo and sent it with his usual perfect aim onto the screen of Armitage's satnav.

'MY SATNAV!' yelled Armitage. 'He's gooed my satnav!'

'Sorry,' said Billy, trying not to laugh.

'I never liked that animal! Not one bit!'

'I think it's mutual,' said Billy.

'In twebblebbnety mebbles, tebble lebble,' said
the satnav.

'He's ruined it! That beast has bust my best
batnav. I mean, satnav.'

Billy felt a jerky tremble rise up into his legs from Narcissus's hump. This, he knew, was a camel cackle. Silent, but unmistakable. Billy squeezed back with his knees, sharing the joke.

On and on they went, rampaging very slowly in the direction of the middle of nowhere, with the satnav gargling out gooey and garbled directions. Armitage gave up on trying to get rid of Narcissus. If life had taught him one thing, it was this: don't mess with that camel. If life had taught him one other thing, it was this: if you *are* going to mess with that camel, make sure you're wearing an ankle-length, goo-proof plastic poncho and a motorbike helmet with the visor down. And Armitage did not have either of those items in his suitcase.

Apart from the occasional cackle practice, Billy and Armitage travelled in silence, both of them lost in thought. Armitage was dreaming of the delicious revenge he was about to wreak on Queenie Bombazine. That woman needed someone to teach her a lesson – drag her back to earth – show her that she wasn't half as special as she thought she was – and Armitage was the man for the job. This, he knew, was going to be His Finest Hour.

Billy, meanwhile, was going over and over in his head the words of the letter hidden in his back pocket. His father was out of jail! He was coming to find him! Billy, finally, was going to be rescued from Armitage and saved from a life of crime. Better than that – better by a thousand times – he was going to see his father again. Armitage needed someone to teach him a lesson, drag him back to earth to show him that he wasn't half as special as he thought he was – and Billy's dad, the great Ernesto Espadrille, was the man for the job.

If Ernesto found his way to the Oh, Wow!

Centre on time, Armitage – for sure – would finally meet his dooooooooooooooom!

✳

Meanwhile, back at the campsite of Shank's Impossible Circus, a meeting was taking place. Hank was banging a hammer on a table.

'I call this meeting to order!' yelled Hank.

'Why should we listen to you?' yelled Frank.

'Because I've got the hammer.'

'It's not your hammer, it's my hammer.'

'Mine.'

'Mine.'

'Get off!'

'You get off!'

'I had it first.'

'*I* had it first. I had it this morning.'

'LISSSSSSSSTEEEEEEEEEEEEEEEEEEEEEN!' boomed Maurice, who was inordinately proud of his booming skills. As a young man, he came second in the annual Loire Valley Amateur Booming Contest, and to this day he was convinced that the winner had cheated. 'Armitage 'as gone on ze rrrrampage wizout us. 'E's up to somesing. 'E's got some snicky plin and 'e's trying to cut us out of ze prrrofits.'

'He's right,' said Irrrrrena, which is what Maurice had told her to say.

'A snicky plin?' said Fingers O'Boyle.

'Yes! Ezzatly!'

'Do you mean a sneaky plan?' asked Fingers.

'Yes! A snicky plin!'

'We can't let him do that,' said Fingers. 'We have to go after him.'

'We can take ze enorrrmous lorry,' said Maurice.

'He's right,' said Irrrrrena.

'I'll drive!' said Hank, who had always wanted to have a go on the enormous lorry.

'No, I'll drive!' said Frank, who had also always

wanted to have a go on the enormous lorry.

'I will!'

'No, I will!'

'No, I will!'

'No, I will!'

'No, I will!'

'No, I will!'

'You'll do what?' said Jesse. 'Where are we going?'

'We're going to rampage after their rampage!' said Fingers. 'Now let's get moving before it's too late!'

EIGHT
The million dollar question[$]

HANNAH AND GRANNY WERE ALSO heading in the direction of the middle of nowhere, though via a different route, which took them over hill and down dale and through forests and along rivers and above crevasses and up cliffs and over mountains and between crags and across lakes and around sinkholes and beneath overhangs and down ski slopes and past bogs and alongside quick-sands and into motorway service stations. Hannah and Granny did not have a satnav.

[$] On the international markets, questions are always priced in dollars. It's a financial tradition. At today's prices, this query is a £621,920 question.

There was one other key difference between Hannah's and Billy's journeys to the Oh, Wow! Centre. Hannah and Granny didn't travel in silence. They chatted and chatted and chatted, in particular about one particular question (the one valued by market experts at £621,920) that had been bothering Hannah ever since the strange details of her origins had been revealed to her.

As always, Hannah got straight to the point.

'Granny,' she said, from the back seat of the mountain tandem, 'something's bothering me. I need to know. Am I a civilian?'

As always, Granny's answer started off heading towards the point before taking a serious diversion to somewhere else entirely. Yes, soon enough it was seaweed and old trainers time, as Granny responded to what seemed like a simple question with a long and complicated rummage through events that happened way back in the olden days. This time, she didn't go back to when Hannah was born, and she didn't go back to when Hannah's mothers were born, she went even further back than that, to when Granny herself was a sprightly young thing, fresh and minty and pure.

'You see, back then I was a trapeze artist myself,' she said.

'You were WHAT?!!!'

'I was an aerial artiste. And not a bad one, either. That's where I met your grandfather, God rest his soul. You never even met him. He was a wonderful man.'

'He was in the circus, too?'

'No, he was an accountant. Like your father. Your father at home, I mean. Not the father we're looking for. But he loved the circus, and when I did a fourteen-night run in Birmingham he came every night and sat in the front row eating a truly enormous candy floss, and as soon as I spotted him

I knew he was the man for me. And he was.'

'What happened to him?'

'Well, he was a very good accountant, but he didn't really want to be. A few years after the twins started school, he decided to chuck in his job and reinvent himself as a tightrope walker. Thing is, balance wasn't his strong point. In fact, he could barely even ride a bike. Which is much more serious when you're a tightrope walker than when you're an accountant. I can't talk about it without feeling weepy and vomitous, but he died doing what he loved, so we must cling to that for comfort.'

'I'm so sorry,' said Hannah. 'I never knew.'

'We kept a lot of things from you, my love. Maybe we shouldn't have. But we thought it would be too much for you when you were small. You see, I gave it all up when I was pregnant with the twins. Until your mother came along, nobody thought pregnancy and trapeze artistry went together. And, of course, once the twins came, I knew I couldn't go back. Part of me wanted to, but it's a hard life with children. Being on the road all the time. And your grandfather had a job. He had to stay put. So I walked away. Left it behind. Or, at least, I thought I did. But when it comes to children, and grandchildren, things from your past have a habit of popping back up again.'

'So Grandad was a civilian, but you're not. You're circus.'

'That's right. I've spent most of my life trying to be a civilian, but it's not really me. In my heart, that's not who I am.'

'But what about your circus friends? Did you just forget about them?'

'I tried to. A few of them visited sometimes, but we mostly drifted apart. They couldn't understand why I chose what I chose, why I married out of the circus, and I don't think I wanted to be reminded of the life that I'd abandoned. There's only one who I stayed close to. She was my protégée, and I still adore her, and you're about to meet her.'

'What's a protégée?'

'It's a young person who's learning to do what you do, and you teach her. Nurture her. Pass down your knowledge to the next generation. It was so long ago, though, that my protégée is middle-aged herself now. She probably has her own protégée. Or is looking for one.'

'Is this . . . ?'

'Queenie Bombazine. From the second I met her, I saw star quality. She hardly knew one end of a trapeze from another back then, but she already had something special. If there were twenty people on stage, it was always her you found yourself looking at. She shone. It was as if she was lit up from the inside. You're going to love her.'

'You still haven't answered my question. Am I a civilian?'

'Strictly speaking, you're a mix. But it always seemed to me it was Grandad's genes that got through to your aunt and mine that went into your mother. Wendy was half civilian, but you'd never know it. Wanda's half circus, but you really wouldn't know that, either. Maybe it hasn't even got anything to do with genes. They just always wanted to be opposites, both of them. The wilder Wendy got, the more cautious Wanda became, and the more cautious Wanda became, the more Wendy wanted to go wild. Siblings are often like that.'

'And my father? I mean my fathers? I mean the one I thought was my father until yesterday is a civilian, but he's not my birth father. And the other two who might be my real father, whichever one it is, they're both circus, aren't they? So I'm circus! I'm almost completely circus!'

'You can't be cut and dried about these things, but I have to say it's always looked to me like that's what you are. Your mother – your aunt-mother – she tried her best to raise you as a civilian, but frankly it was an uphill struggle. And it really didn't take, did it?'

'I knew it! **KERCHOO** it! **BAZOO IT! HULLABALOO** it!' All her life Hannah had felt somehow *different*, in a way that always worried her. She found it hard to concentrate at school, hard to concentrate at home, and even quite hard to concentrate on walking from home to school and back again. Nothing clicked. But now Granny had told her she really was different – different in the precise way she most wanted to be different – and this was the most joyous, uplifting, thrilling relief.

In all the excitement of having her dearest wish confirmed, Hannah found it almost impossible to sit still.

'Hannah, dear, why don't you get down. I don't think tandems are designed to be ridden by standing on the saddle,' said Granny, patiently.

'What about like this?'

'That's very good, but I don't think standing on one leg makes it any safer.'

'Safety shmafety. I'm going to try a handstand.'

Granny pedalled on wearily. She'd seen it all before, twenty or so years earlier, on this very tandem, with Hannah's mother.

It was following an unhappy tandem ride shared by the twins, during which Wendy had insisted on attempting a tandem wheelie down a staircase, that Wanda had decided on a career in health and safety enforcement.

The twins, after that day, were never close. Even once Wanda was out of her casts, she never really trusted Wendy again.

But, of course, Wanda did raise her child. Because however hard it is to get on, however different you may be, a sister is still a sister.

So Hannah and Granny pedalled onwards, towards the Oh, Wow! Centre, Hannah's heart beating to a new, jazzy beat now that she knew she was circus. It had been a quite extraordinary birthday. She had learned that her mother wasn't her mother; that she had an aunt she never even knew existed who was actually her real mother; that her real mother was dead; that her granny was a former trapeze artist; and that Billy was either her brother or her half-brother. It was all rather a lot to take in.

'This must be rather a lot to take in,' said

Granny, sympathetically.

Freaky.

'Are you a mind-reader, too?' said Hannah, who did not like the idea of this one little bit.

'No, dear,' said Granny, 'I just know what you're thinking.'

'Then you are a mind-reader.'

Granny stopped the bike and turned to face Hannah. 'I'm not, because I can only do it with you, and I can only do it sometimes,' she replied, looking at her through those penetrating blue eyes that Hannah suddenly realised were exactly like her own. Granny smiled, with lips that Hannah noticed were strikingly similar to her own lips, and the chunky tandem fell to the ground as the two of them toppled into a big, soppy hug. In among all the crazy and exciting and weird and scary changes that had crashed into Hannah's life today, the most important thing she had learned was that Granny was still her granny.

'Yuk!' shouted the bike. 'Hugs!!! I hate hugs!
Stop it right now or I'll do a big chunky puke
on your shoes.'

They ignored the bike and
finished their hug.

'I'm all muddy now,' ranted
the bike, 'but I don't even care!
I can't even feel it. I could be
ten times as muddy as
this and I wouldn't
even feel a thing!'

Granny then did
something surprising. She
dashed to the nearest tree,
faster than Hannah had ever
seen her move, scampered up the
trunk, tiptoed to the end of a long, high
branch, jumped off, caught the branch
with her hands, swung back, then

forward, then back, then all the way round, before letting go, somersaulting through the air, and landing neatly in front of Hannah.

Hannah's mouth opened, but no sound came out.

Granny picked up the bike and got on. 'I'm terribly out of practice,' she said, 'but it's fun to dust off the old skills once in a while.'

'Why didn't you tell me? Why didn't you show me before?' stammered Hannah.

'Oh, the past is the past,' replied Granny, casually. 'No point dwelling on things.'

'That was *incredible*!'

Granny shrugged, and off they went.

After a short while, the bike chipped in, sulkily, 'I could do that. If I had hands. Easy. No sweat.'

The middle of nowhere becomes the centre of everything

THE MIDDLE OF NOWHERE PREPARED carefully for Queenie Bombazine's arrival. Kelvin Pype had ensured that no stone was left unturned in getting everything perfect for the arrival of his heroine. As soon as he took the booking, he'd called a meeting for all the staff and said to them: 'Big news! Queenie Bombazine's coming to perform! Go outside and turn over all the stones!'

After the mammoth stone-turning exercise,

there were lots of other arrangements to arrange, preparations to prepare, plans to plan, measures to measure, fixings to fix and organs to organise. The finest suite in the Oh, Wow! hotel was set aside and plumbed in with three extra baths; a football-pitch-sized area of car park was cordoned off for Queenie's vans, caravans, vanacans and vanacanavanacanavans; the seating was rearranged to point towards a ring in the middle of the arena; lighting was rigged up; sound was checked; 🔖 and everybody went for a haircut, because they all wanted to look super-good when they met the legendary aerialiste. Most importantly, of course, the Oh, Wow! Centre was flooded.

Don't worry. I'm not talking about one of those pesky natural floods where streets turn into rivers and rivers turn into raging torrents and raging torrents

---

🔖 Before all performances of any kind, sound is always checked. This involves a man in a black T-shirt that is too large and black jeans that are too small muttering '1-2-3 testing 1-2-3,' into each microphone while a man at the back of the hall in similar clothes shouts back something along the lines of, 'Yes, that sounds like sound.' These people live according to mysterious rules known only to them and are rarely seen in daylight.

just go nuts. No, I mean flooded in the sense of being filled with water on purpose. Not right to the top. The seats all stayed above water. The stage alone was transformed into a giant, glass-sided swimming pool. Because, as you may recall, this was no ordinary circus – it was Queenie Bombazine's Ecstatic Aquatic Splashtastic Circus of the Century. And, while it is perfectly possible to be ecstatic in the dry, for the aquatic and splashtastic elements of the show, water was a necessity. It was the essence of what made Queenie's show unique. Queenie was fabulous in every single department of fabulousness, but a star cannot rest on her fabulousness alone. In the circus world, you need a gimmick, and water was Queenie's.

When she arrived and saw Kelvin's work, Queenie politely ignored the fact that every stone in sight was upside down, and told him that his preparations were fantastic. She was so pleased, she gave him an enormous kiss on the cheek (a kiss that, as it happens, he thought about every single day for the next fifty-eight years, until he died a contented, peaceful death, moments after blowing out the candles on his 100th birthday cake).

'It's s-s-s-such a p-p-p-pleasure to see you again,' said Kelvin, who was doing a poor job of disguising his nervousness. 'I'm so excited about the sh-sh-show.'

'My sea lions need their water changed,' said Queenie, which was not the reply Kelvin was expecting. He had hoped that the hug might lead to some kind of friendly chat, but this was not Queenie's way, at least not when there was work to do. 'Could you possibly lend me a hose, a bucket, a pair of waders and a colander?'

'I . . . I'll get them right away.'

'And a gin fizz.'

'OK.'

'That's for me, not the sea lions.'

'Of course. And I thought you might want to know that we've installed some extra baths in the hotel's presidential suite.'

'Thank you so much. I'm going to be knee-deep in sea-lion poo for the next half-hour, but after that, a bath will be just the ticket.'

The roar of a motorbike engine signalled the arrival of Reginald Clench, who dismounted from his bike, removed a brown leather crash helmet with built-in goggles, and marched towards Kelvin Pype. Literally marched. He stopped with a firm stamp and shook Kelvin's hand.

'Pype!' said Clench.

'Clench,' said Pype.

'Absolutely. AtennnSHUN!'

Kelvin stood to attention.

'Not you, private. The dog.'

Kelvin looked down. At their feet was a dog, standing rigidly upright on its two hind legs, like a meerkat. But it wasn't a meerkat. It was a mere dog. It was Rudolph.

'At ease!' snapped Clench.

The dog lay down. Clench turned to Pype. 'Fine to see you, Pype, what what, and all that nonsense. Onwards and upwards. No time like the present. Let's get cracking. Charts are here – lighting cues, sound cues, set, safety rig, timings, costume requirements, dressing-room requirements, other requirements, sundries, extras, expenses, etc. I'll give you thirty-five minutes to peruse and digest, then I'll chair a meeting. I want all the relevant teams. No lateness, no slackness, no interruptions, no trainers, no loose talk or sloppy posture. Pip pip. Things to do. See you in thirty-four and a half minutes.'

And off he marched. Literally. Rudolph followed,

perfectly in step, one pace behind.

'He's a wonder,' said Queenie. 'Isn't he?'

'Oh, yes,' said Kelvin. 'A wonder.'

✴

By the time Clench's meeting was finished and the animals were settled and the stage was prepared and the lighting was perfected and the sound re-checked, the Ecstatic Aquatic Splashtastic Circus of the Century had run out of time. The audience was already arriving. For almost the first time in the history of the Oh, Wow! Centre, the show would have to start without a dress rehearsal.

This had only ever happened once before when a rock band went out to the pub, then forgot what city they were in and got lost for six hours, only to return in a very unfocused frame of mind five minutes before curtain-up. That notorious occasion had given Kelvin a stomach ulcer which took several months to heal.

This time, he wasn't worried. Well, he was worried, because he was always worried. He ate worry for breakfast, from a worry-bowl with a worry-spoon, accompanied by worry-tea and worry-on-toast. But, over and above the usual background anxiety, Kelvin trusted Queenie Bombazine more than he trusted any other artiste to have set foot on his stage.

She was a legend. Most stars these days weren't proper stars – they were just skinny people with lollipop heads and good teeth who looked good on telly – but Queenie was different. She was the real thing.

Kelvin, for no good reason, and against all his principles, felt confident.

Queenie wouldn't fail him.

Billy's low point

TURGABURBLE LEBEBBLE OBOBBONTO thobble B983,' said Armitage's satnav. The burble was getting worse. As Billy and Armitage made the final turning of their very slow rampage, a thrilling sight appeared on the horizon.

Yes. A huge and pointless tent. The Oh, Wow! Centre.

'Look!' cried Billy. 'It's the middle of nowhere! At last!'

Armitage smiled, which was approximately as

hard for the muscles of his face as it is for an average human to do three hundred press-ups. Smiling was right near the top of the list of Activities That Armitage Did Roughly Once A Year. 📱

What drew Armitage's eye was not the huge and pointless tent, but the array of vans, caravans, vanacans and vanacanavanacanavans in the car park, the largest of which was emblazoned with the words 'Queenie Bombazine's Ecstatic Aquatic Splashtastic Circus'.

'Ha!' said Armitage, which was the smallest cackle he could manage. 'Splashtastic! That's not even a word!'

'Isn't it?' said Billy. 'It makes me think of frolics andexcitementandfantasticwateryentertainments.'

'Well, it shouldn't. It should make you think of going out and buying that show-offy woman a dictionary and a tin of paint and suggesting that she correct her advertising so as not to lead

---

📱 That list in full: 1. Being honest. 2. Smiling. 3. Being polite. 4. Playing badminton.

vulnerable youth into the clutches of eccentric and irregular vocabulary.'

'Is show-offy a word?'

Armitage's moustache began to twitch, which is what happened when he sensed someone might be getting the better of him.

'Listen to me, young man,' he snapped. 'I don't want any of your lip. You're either with me or against me. Do you hear? Now which is it?'

'I can't remember,' said Billy.

'DON'T MAKE JOKES! I HATE JOKES! JOKES ARE FOR STUPID PEOPLE WHO CAN'T THINK OF ANYTHING SENSIBLE TO SAY, AND NO SON OF MINE HAS THE RIGHT TO BE STUPID! DO YOU HEAR ME?'

'PSSSSSSSSSSSSSSSSSSSSSSSSSSSSSSSSSSSSSSSSSS SSSSSSSSSSSSSSSSSSSSSSSSSSSSSSSSSSSSS SSSSSSSSSSSSSSSSSSSSSS SSSSSSS SSS S S S S,' said Narcissus, and not with his mouth.

'He's splashed my shoes!' said Armitage. 'Can't you keep that beast under control?'

'Yes, Father,' said Billy, who had decided this was a good moment to stop being cheeky. Narcissus, he felt, had done a pretty unbeatable job of winning the argument for him.

They rode the rest of the way to the Oh, Wow! Centre in silence, and arrived with two hours to spare before the show.

Armitage deposited Billy at a café in the enormous shopping centre that ran all round the Oh, Wow! Centre, told him not to move, and ordered an apple juice for him.

'Does that come in extra-extra small?' Armitage asked the waitress, employing what he thought was a charming smile, but was in fact a dismal and terrifying leer that gave her nightmares for two weeks.

While Billy sipped his minuscule juice, Armitage tiptoed around the Oh, Wow! Centre, examining things through a pair of binoculars.

Examining what?

I'm sure you can guess. Vans, caravans, vanacans, and vanacanavanacanavans and, above all, Reginald Clench's Portakabin box office.▰

When Armitage returned from his recce, his eyes were alight with a gleam that Billy recognised,

---

▰ A box office, contrary to logic, is not an office filled with boxes. It is a place from which tickets are sold and, more importantly for the purposes of our story, a place in which the money raised by ticket sales is kept. Yes, Armitage was a-plotting. Dastardly deeds were afoot.

a gleam fired by greed, determination and malice stewed together into a mulch of soupy, stinking wickedness. It was such a hideous gleam it was like bad breath of the eyeballs. You couldn't look at him without a flip-flop of discomfort flop-flipping in your tummy.

Armitage ordered himself an extra large cappa-frappa-mocha-tocha-lochaccino with chocolate sprinkles and cinnamon sprinkles and extra sugar sprinkled on the sprinkles and extra sprinkles sprinkled on the sugar. He sat down opposite Billy, peered over the top of his bucket-sized drink and whispered, 'I have a plan!'

'Oh, good,' said Billy, thinking, *Oh, bad.*

'We have tickets for both nights. Tonight, we scope things out. Tomorrow, we strike!'

'I didn't know burglars went on strike.'

'No! We strike! We make our move! We hit Queenie for all the takings!'

'Oh. OK.'

'This is going to be the biggest bonanza ever! It's going to be my masterstroke!'

'You say that every time.'

'Do I?'

'Yes.'

'Well, it's important to be optimistic. It keeps you young. '**HahahahahahaHAHAHAHAHA!**'

This time, Billy recognised the cackle and tried to join in. '**HahahahahahaHAHAHAHAHA!**' he replied.

'You've got it!' yelped Armitage, spooning cappa-frappa-mocha-tocha-lochaccino froth into his mouth, which gave him a moustache of froth on top of his moustache of moustache, and a moustache of chocolate sprinkles on top of the moustache of froth, and a moustache of cinnamon sprinkles on top of the moustache of chocolate sprinkles, and a moustache of sugar on top of the moustache of cinnamon sprinkles. The quintuple moustache look was a new one, fashion-wise, but Armitage pulled it off.

Billy smiled wanly, wishing the same wish he had wished more or less every day of his life. But today it was pulsing through him more powerfully than ever, because now, for the first time, he had a glimmer of hope that it might actually happen. *If only my father would come! If only my father would come!*

'Maybe I can turn you into a good little thief after all,' said Armitage, reaching forwards and, in a moment of rare affection, pinching Billy's cheek between finger and thumb. (I'm using the word 'affection' very loosely here, to include actions which are annoying, humiliating and physically painful.)

Billy looked down at his very small, very empty cup. *If only!* he kept on thinking. *If only my father would appear now and save me from this multiple-moustached monster. I don't want to be a thief! I don't want to be a Shank! I want to be an Espadrille!*

Billy was having a low point.

As the crowds around him hurrying towards the circus swelled, thousands of people all out for the night of their lives, Billy felt more alone than ever. A hubbub of excitement echoed around the vast concourse of the arena as more and more people arrived, while Billy felt nothing but sorrow, loneliness and gloom.

What chance did his father stand of finding him here? Even if Ernesto did find his way to the Oh, Wow! Centre, how on earth would he locate Billy in among all these people? What hope was there that anyone would ever find him and help him?

There is one good thing about low points. If a low point really is a low point, from there, the only way is up.

Speaking of which, just as Billy was feeling more alone than ever, a girl was arriving in the very same building, accompanied by her granny. Billy had no idea she was there. Not yet. He also had no idea that she was looking for him. And of course, more significantly, he had no idea that this granny was also his granny. Nor that the girl was his sister.

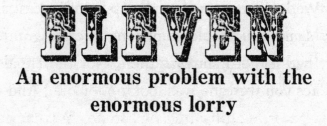

ELEVEN

An enormous problem with the enormous lorry

'SLUGGASLUGGACHAPFFFFUTPFFFF ffutpffffffffffffffffffffutpffffffffffffffffffffffffffffffffff fffffffffffffffffffffffffffffffffffffffffffffffffffffffffffffff ffffffffftkch,' said the enormous lorry, lurching to a sudden and unexpected stop.

A long, worried silence filled the cabin.

'What was that?' said Hank.

'I don't know,' said Frank. 'We've stopped.'

'Oh, really? I hadn't noticed.'

'You hadn't noticed?'

'Of course I'd noticed! I was being sarcastic.'

'Well, maybe you should stop being sarcastic.'

'Maybe *you* should stop being sarcastic.'

'I wasn't being sarcastic.'

'Yes you were.'

'No I wasn't.'

'What's going on?' said Maurice.

'Maurice is right,' said Irrrrrena, jolting awake from a doze.

'Why have we stopped?' said Fingers.

'I don't know,' said Hank.

'I don't know, either,' said Frank.

'It's the engine,' said Jesse.

'OBVIOUSLY IT'S THE ENGINE,' said Hank and Frank and Maurice and Irrrrrena and Fingers.

'It's got no petrol left,' said Jesse.

'What???!' said Hank and Frank and Maurice and Irrrrrena and Fingers.

'Look at the petrol gauge,' said Jesse. 'It's empty. I've been worrying about it all day.'

'Why didn't you say something!?' snapped Hank and Frank and Maurice and Irrrrrena and Fingers.

'Nobody asked me,' said Jesse.

'YOU IDIOT!' yelled Hank and Frank and

Maurice and Irrrrrena and Fingers.

'I'm not an idiot. I'm just shy. And if *I'm* the idiot, how come I'm the only one who noticed we were running out of petrol?'

'You're an idiot, because you didn't *say* we were running out of petrol,' said Hank and Frank and Maurice and Irrrrrrrena and Fingers.

'Well maybe I didn't say anything because every time I speak, you all shout at me.'

'YOU'RE AN IDIOT!' shouted Hank and Frank and Maurice and Irrrrrena and Fingers.

'Right! That's it! I'm going to sulk in the back!'

Jesse climbed out of the cabin and went for his sulk.

The others stared at the petrol gauge. The petrol gauge stared back, with an empty expression on its face.

There was another long silence.

'Why didn't you put any petrol in?' yelled

Frank, eventually.

'Why didn't *you* put any petrol in?' yelled Hank.

'STOOOOOOOP   IIIIIIIIIIIIIIIIIT!'   yelled
Irrrrrena. 'I've had enough of your bickering.
Enough! I can't take it any more. I'm going to go in
the back and sulk with Jesse.'

'She's right,' said Maurice. 'Me, too.'

'And me,' said Fingers.

'And me,' said Frank.

'Fine!' said Hank, calling after them. 'I'll stay
here and sulk on my own. In the front. Where it's
more comfortable. So there. I'm going to have the
comfiest sulk ever. Think about that!'

And this is where the rampage after the rampage
ended, with a circus of sulkers stuck in the slow
lane of the B764, just a mile and a half short of the
middle of nowhere.

'OOH, I'M SO COMFY!' shouted Hank. 'I'M
LYING DOWN NOW.'

Frank's muffled but angry voice rose up from the back of the enormous lorry. 'JUST BE QUIET!'

'I THINK I'LL PUT THE RADIO ON,' replied Hank. 'OOH, MUSIC! HOW LOVELY!'

TWELVE
Opening night

WHEN HANNAH WALKED INTO THE OH, Wow! Centre auditorium, she said the only thing you can say when you walk into the Oh, Wow! Centre auditorium. She said, 'Oh, Wow!'

The Oh, Wow! Centre auditorium❡ is enormous. So enormous that, having entered at the back, it was still a long walk to Hannah's seat, which was at the very front, in the very middle, with lots of legroom and even a cushion specially shaped for posh bottoms. This was the best seat in the house.

❡ I like the word auditorium. It comes from the Latin words audit, meaning 'very expensive', and orium, meaning 'a place where ice cream is'.

But Hannah soon forgot how good her seat was, because once the show started she forgot everything about everything. She was, quite simply, mesmerised.

✷

Billy, only a minute or two after Hannah, also walked into the Oh, Wow! auditorium, and he, too, said the only thing you can say when you walk into the Oh, Wow!, except that for him it was a very short walk from the entrance to his seat at the back, which had no legroom and no cushion and as much view of the stage as a birdwatcher might get of a migrating goose. This was the worst seat in the house.

But Billy soon forgot how bad his seat was, because once the show started he forgot everything about everything. He was, quite simply, mesmerised.

✷

First up was Cissy Noodles and her swimming poodles, though to call them swimming poodles is to seriously underplay their talents, because they also dived, leapt, danced, barked amusing arrangements of popular songs, played underwater snooker and rode a motorised surfboard in an arrangement that is usually called a human pyramid, but in this case was a poodle pyramid.

After that came the Aquabats of Arabia, seven of them, all of whom seemed to have only a loose acquaintance with the laws of gravity. They flew through the air, darted through the water, and flung each other from one element to the other in a series of manoeuvres that made them seem weightless and amphibian and impossibly strong and perfectly balanced and essentially like a troupe of exquisitely choreographed man-bird-fishes. They did this dressed in costumes so tight-fitting that it didn't seem like they were wearing any costume at all, except for the fact that sometimes it looked like skin, sometimes like glistening scales, sometimes like feathers.

When they left the stage, to the sound of uproarious, roof-lifting applause, more than half the audience turned to the person next to them and asked, 'Did that just happen? Were they human?'

Next up was Bunny Weasel and her synchronised otters. If you've never seen a synchronised otter show, the important thing to understand here is that it's pretty much what it sounds like. Otters. Synchronised. But you have to see this to know how incredibly cute it is. Because even otters out of synch are cute. In synch, the whole thing just goes off the top of the cuteness chart. 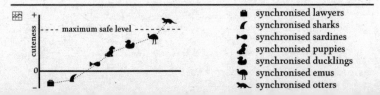 The otters' tea party with which Bunny finished her act usually resulted in several audience-member faintings. Tonight was no exception, and ambulance crews were on hand at all the exits with cute-attack revival kits (i.e. buckets of cold water).

After that was Ruggles Pynchon, who did such

synchronised lawyers
synchronised sharks
synchronised sardines
synchronised puppies
synchronised ducklings
synchronised emus
synchronised otters

an extraordinary disappearing act that the collective gasp was so loud, it made a passing meteorologist send out a hurricane warning.

I won't go through the whole show, because that will just make you jealous that you missed it, but I must describe to you the final act, which was, of course, Queenie Bombazine herself.

Normal trapeze artists swing from a trapeze. Queenie didn't seem to do this. The trapeze was there – it was part of the act – but she hardly needed it. She appeared to fly through the air all of her own accord, backwards and forwards, twisting and flipping and somersaulting and swirling without ever seeming to need the trapeze to catch or propel her. And, of course, there was also the diving and swimming, the way she moved through water like a dolphin, never using her arms, needing only ripples of movement through her torso and legs to zoom her wherever she wanted to go.

Everything she did looked at the same time utterly impossible and totally effortless.

So breathtaking was her performance that some members of the audience literally forgot to breathe, leading to more faintings and emergency revivals.

The whole show was extraordinary, but since

circuses are supposed to be extraordinary, you could say that the extraordinariness of the show was in fact rather ordinary. Apart from one thing. One moment. A moment that for everyone in the audience except Billy was entirely ordinary (in the extraordinary/ordinary way I've just explained). It happened towards the end of the act, when high up in the air above the stage, swinging to and fro with angelic grace, Queenie reached out and grabbed a dangling mirrorball. This was the only movement she made that wasn't perfectly smooth. Something about it seemed improvised, unrehearsed, slightly jerky. Queenie only held the mirrorball for a second, but while she had it in her grasp, she moved it into a spotlight and positioned it at a very deliberate angle.

What was so deliberate about this angle? Well, it sent a shaft of reflected light downwards, towards one particular seat in the front row, where a girl was sitting. This girl blinked in the glare and shielded her face, but not too quickly for Billy to recognise her.

This, Billy knew, was a message – a secret message – intended just for him. How he knew it, he didn't know, but sometimes we all know things without knowing how we know them, and this was one of those times.

'Oh, my giddy aunt!' yelled Billy, leaping to his feet. 'It's . . .'

Luckily, just as this moment of pure joy was on the brink of shattering all his inhibitions, Billy remembered who was sitting next to him. With enormous effort, just in time, he silenced himself, wiped the grin from his features, and sat down.

'It's what?' snapped Armitage.

Billy had to think fast. Armitage could not be allowed to know that Hannah was there. He was in the middle of a revenge rampage, and Hannah was right near the top of Armitage's list of People Who Need To Be Taken Down A Peg Or Two. She had diddled him, stitched him up, done him like a kipper, and Armitage did not enjoy being diddled, stitched or kippered, not one little bit. All diddlers, stitchers and kipperers went straight onto Armitage's list, and the only way to get off it was to be diddled, stitched or kippered back.

The last thing Billy wanted to do was to let Armitage know of Hannah's presence.

'It's . . . cold,' said Billy.

'No it isn't,' replied Armitage.

'I mean it's hot.'

'You're right. Too stingy to put the air conditioning on, probably. Typical. That's Queenie all over. All mouth and no trousers. All gong and no dinner. All frills and feathers and fancy fripperies, but no ventilation to keep the punters comfortable. Am I right or am I right?'

'You're right,' said Billy. 'Typical.'

Billy tutted supportively, but inside he was very much not tutting. In his heart, he was skippling, zooping and jiggiemuffering⬭ for joy. Hannah, his friend and saviour, was there! Right there!

Unfortunately, so were ten thousand other people. He'd seen her, but now he had to get to her, which might not be so simple.

'Time to go,' said Armitage, grabbing Billy's arm and hauling him towards the exit.

'But the show isn't over!'

'We're not here to have fun! We're working!' said Armitage. 'Anyway, it's all hype if you ask me. Boring, in my opinion. Average at best.'

Together, they sneaked out of the auditorium and headed towards a vantage point concealed behind a thick pillar, from where they had an unobstructed view of the box office. It was from this spot that Armitage watched, with particular

---

⬭ What do you mean, 'that's not in the dictionary'? Pah! Dictionaries are overrated. Or should that be over-rated? I'll have to look it up.

interest, the moment when Reginald Clench left the ticket desk and locked up, before walking towards the stage carrying a tuba, for his part in the finale. This was Clench's only self-indulgence. He couldn't resist claiming just a sliver of the limelight, by providing the *oompah* for the last tune of the show, dressed as a Hawaiian maiden, floating across the stage on an inflatable palm tree.🌴

When Clench was on stage, who was in the box office, guarding the safe?

Armitage took out his binoculars. He was drooling.

Billy knew that look on his face. With a little less self-control, Armitage would have been cackling, too. This was the look of a dastardly scheme falling into place.

🌴 If you're only going to have one indulgence in life, why not this one? I can't see anything wrong with it. If I worked for a circus, knew how to play the tuba, and looked good in a grass skirt, I'd probably do the exact same thing. Whether or not Reginald Clench looked good in a grass skirt is open to debate.

THIRTEEN

Backstage at the Oh, Wow!

AFTER THE SHOW, Granny took Hannah backstage. The circus on its own was almost more excitement than Hannah could take, so the idea of actually meeting the circussers afterwards was close to mind-blowing.

What a birthday! Even though she'd only been given two presents – a chunky tandem and a filing cabinet – this was still proving to be the best birthday of her life.

Hannah gripped Granny's hand as they edged

through the thick■ crowd of circus-watchers heading happily home. Granny's hand was both gnarled (because she was old) and sticky (because she'd been scoffing candy floss for the last two hours), but it felt to Hannah like the most comforting thing in the world. Granny had always been an important person to Hannah, but now more than ever. She was her link to the past, to the mystery of her parentage and to her long-lost mother. Crowds usually scared Hannah, who preferred fresh air, grassy meadows and the feel of cowpats squelching underfoot, but as long as she had a grip of her sticky, gnarled grandmother, she felt safe.

After several conversations with sour-faced security men who all sprouted curly wires out of their ears and down into the back of their suits (which made them look as if they had battery-powered brains (which maybe they did)) Hannah

---

■ That's thick as in lots of them close together, not thick as in stupid. Maybe some of them were a bit thick, but that's not important right now.

and Granny were ushered into a long corridor with a thick ■ red carpet.

Somehow, Granny knew where to go. The further they walked through the winding passageways of the Oh, Wow! backstage area, the tighter Granny gripped Hannah's hand. There was a look on Granny's face Hannah had never seen before – a gleam in her eye, a flush to her cheeks, and a slight tremble in the loose flappy bits on her neck. Despite being old and gnarled and sticky, her grandmother was clearly just as excited by circussiness as Hannah.

'Granny?' said Hannah.

Granny stopped walking and gave Hannah's hand an extra squeeze. 'I know,' said Granny.

That was the end of the conversation – a conversation which perhaps appears totally meaningless – but which to Hannah and Granny made perfect sense. They were telling one another

---

■ That's thick as in deep, not thick as in stupid. This carpet was, in fact, of unusually high intelligence.

this was almost too much excitement to bear, and checking the other one felt the same thing – a feeling like that of simultaneously skydiving, winning the lottery, and needing a pee really, really badly.

After this exceptionally concise chat, they both felt reassured that the feeling was mutual.

Gripping hands tighter than ever, they arrived at a door with a large star on it and the thrilling words: '✫QUEENIE BOMBAZINE✫ – **DO NOT DISTURB**'. Maybe the last three words weren't particularly exciting, but the first two more than made up for it. This was her dressing room! Queenie Bombazine! Living legend! Mermaid of the Skies! Etc.!

Granny knocked noisily with her gnarled knuckles.[†]

'Mmm-hmmm?' came the reply, which sounded like a 'come in', but with a hint of 'though I'd

---

[†] How I wish that could be knocked gnoisily with her gnarled knuckles! If only we could fit a knight's knitted knapsack of gnome's knickers into this scene! Don't you sometimes just love kpointless gletters?

prefer you to go away'.

They went in. The first thing that hit Hannah was the smell. Or, rather, the scent. This was the most perfumed room she had ever visited. Entering Queenie's dressing room was like diving into a swimming pool of rose petals; it was like smacking yourself in the face with a mallet of loveliness; it was a grenade of exquisite, wafty fabulosity exploding inside your nostrils.

One moment Queenie was sitting at her dressing table, the next she was on top of them, squealing with delight, hugging Granny, then hugging Hannah, then hugging both of them at once, so hard that they both lifted off the floor. She may have looked dainty up on that trapeze, but this was a woman with serious muscles. Hannah had never been hugged like this in her whole life. Her mother's hugs were ticklish, dainty, fluttery things that felt like being delicately wrapped in a gauze curtain.

This hug was more like a cross between a full body massage from two massive silken cushions and how the last few moments of your life might feel before you were gobbled up by a wild bear.

If Hannah's mother had been there, she would have no doubt tried to stop the whole thing, chipping in with an 'Oooh! Goodness! Careful of her little bones.' But Queenie was not careful, and she clearly had scant regard for the supposed fragility of young skeletons.

Hannah prided herself on being independent and self-reliant, but in Queenie's arms she felt an entirely new and strangely delicious sensation of being almost swallowed up by someone big and strong and competent and generally overflowing with wonderfulness. Even though they were almost strangers, Hannah felt as if this was possibly the best hug she had ever been given.

Everybody needs hugs, just like everybody needs to drink. Hannah's mother did hug her, and also gave her glasses of diluted juice whenever she asked for them, but hugging Queenie was like leaping under a waterfall.

Sometimes, when you are overwhelmed by a situation, the strangest things come out of your mouth. This is what happened to Hannah. The first words she ever spoke to Queenie Bombazine were these: 'Can I feel your muscles?'

This could have easily proved embarrassing. As I'm sure you know, 'Can I feel your muscles?' isn't your average greeting. But Queenie wasn't the kind of person who cared for average greetings. In fact, she seemed rather pleased by Hannah's question.

'Of course,' she said, clenching her bicep for Hannah.

Hannah had a good squeeze, with one hand, then two. It was like rock.

'Can I feel yours?' said Queenie.

'OK,' said Hannah. 'They're not very good yet. I'm only twelve.'

Hannah clenched. Queenie felt.

'Not bad,' said Queenie. 'Your mother was a skinny thing, but she was strong, too.'

These words zapped at Hannah's heart, sending an electric jolt through her whole body. Her mouth opened and shut, like a fish. This couldn't be her home-mother Queenie was talking about – the be-careful-don't-forget-your-scarf mother – this was her *real* mother.

'You knew my mother!' said Hannah.

'Of course I did. She was my protégée.'

'But I thought you were Granny's proto . . . whatsit . . . thingamajig.'

'I was. I was Granny's protégée. She taught me everything. Then Esmeralda – Wendy – your mum – she was my protégée. All the secrets of how to be a superstar aerialiste went straight from mother to daughter, via me.'

Hannah's mouth was still doing the fish thing. Her head was filled with more questions than ever, but she couldn't get a sound to come out of her mouth.

'You must have a thousand questions for me,' said Queenie, who recognised a case of fish-mouth when she saw one, 'but let's sit down and have a nice cuppa first. What do you say to that? Me and your granny have got a lot of catching up to do. Pop?'

'Pardon?'

'Pop?'

'Have you got hiccups?'

'No. Pop?'

'Er . . . why do you keep saying pop? Is this a game?'

'It's an old-fashioned word for fizzy drinks,' said Granny. 'She's offering you a fizzy drink.'

'Oh!' said Hannah. 'No thanks. I'm not allowed fizzy drinks. My mother says they're bad for you.'

'She's right, they are bad for you. Now live a

little and wrap your gums round that,' said Queenie, passing her a bottle of lurid orange liquid.

Hannah sipped.

It was really quite spectacularly revolting, with a taste of floor polish, burnt toffee and plastic oranges, but she smiled politely and said, 'Thank you.'

✗

Meanwhile, not far away, not far away at all, Billy was circling the concourse of the arena, pushing through the crowds, searching frantically for Hannah, scouring every child's face, hunting desperately, but in vain.

She was there, of course, right there, but he was not going to find her. Not tonight.

Luckily (and cleverly), Billy had remembered one useful thing from their last encounter. He had a strong memory of looking up at her during his performance, while doing some archery from

Narcissus's back, and seeing not just Hannah and her granny, but also the two largest sticks of candy floss he had ever clapped eyes on. This tiny factoid represented his last hope.

Of course, most people go to the circus then go home. Most people go once. But Hannah, he knew, was not most people and nor was her granny.

By the time the arena was empty, Billy had formed a right-next-door-to-completely-hopeless plan. He had a sensation that was somewhere between a vague instinct and a wild guess that Hannah and her granny might come back for the second night. And, if they did, he had an idea where he'd find them.

The candy floss stall.

He had very nearly given up. But not quite. And that tiny glimmer of hope, of determination and intelligence and willpower, was to change everything.

A factoid is a very small fact. A facticle is a very small factoid. A factini is a very small facticle. You can fit two hundred and seventy-three factinis on a pinhead.

Queenie drained her tea and turned to Hannah. 🖜

'So,' she said. 'This takes me back.'

Hannah had forced down a third of her pop, which gave her furry teeth, a claggy tongue, and a stomach that now thought it was a hot-air balloon. If she wanted a similar sensation again, next time she'd skip the pop and just squirt a fire extinguisher into her mouth. ⚠ 'Back to what?' she said.

'Back to the first time I met your mother. She hated pop, too.'

'I don't hate it. I just think it's not really my thing.'

'And, like you, she had good manners.'

'Oh.'

'And intelligent eyes.'

'Really?'

'I see a lot of her in you. But you also seem like your own person. She was too, of course, so that

---

🖜 You see what I did there, don't you? I skipped the cup of tea – the bit where Queenie has a good old catch-up with Granny – because who wants to listen to a couple of old people banging on about the olden days, eh? Nobody. Not me, not you, not Little Boy Blue or Jimmy Choo or the mayor of Timbuktu.

⚠ Health and safety announcement for very stupid people. Don't do this. Actually, come to think of it, if you are stupid enough to want to do this, you should probably go ahead and get it done, because it's only a matter of time before you wipe yourself out in some act of catastrophic denseness or other, so it might as well be this one.

makes you like her as well.'

'I see.' Hannah wanted to know everything about her mother, but she couldn't think where to start.

'Was she nice?' she said, which was such a dull thing to ask it hadn't even been on her mental list of questions, but, as I'm sure you know, the moments in life when it is most important to say the right thing are exactly the same moments when your mouth is most likely to shoot off in a random direction and spout a load of old claptrap. Mouths are like that: unpredictable, verging on naughty, verging on downright rebellious.

'Nice? *Nice? NICE?*' replied Queenie, her considerable chest bulging with outrage.

'Was she not nice?' Hannah asked, worried now.

'Nice isn't the word. Nice doesn't even come close. Your mother was ... she was a force of nature. She was generous with her heart and her laughter and her time and her money and her spirit; she was a fighter and a listener and a performer and a worker and a dreamer and imaginative and inspiring and funny and serious and intelligent and silly and warm and also just incredibly cool and on stage she was luminous with beauty. But it wasn't mirror-beauty, it wasn't photograph-beauty, it was something inside her, something in her eyes and her mouth and the way she looked at you, or the way she smiled, or the way she didn't smile; it's impossible to describe her, because you can't compare her to anyone else and it's very, very sad that she died, but life is full of sad things, and I know that of everything she achieved or could have achieved, nothing – nothing – would ever have come close to the fact that she made you. And meeting you has been pure joy, because now I can see that even though she is gone, in a way she isn't gone at all. Her spirit and beauty and life-force is right here, fully alive, in you.'

Silent tears began to roll down Hannah's cheeks, tears that were both happy and sad and ecstatic and doom-laden and every other emotion in between.

Queenie enveloped her in another of those colossal hugs. 'You let it all out, dear,' she said, stroking her back, and Hannah did just that. She let it all out.

Hannah wept and wept. Granny wept and wept. Queenie wept and wept. You can insert your own sound-effects here, depending on the thickness of your walls, the proximity of sleeping babies, and your level of enthusiasm for putting on a show, but something along the lines of 'HUBBAHUBBAGLEEUUURKGLEEUUURK UBABABOOOOHOOOOBOOOOGOOOO DOOOOO-HAGUB-HAGUB-GLIFFGLIFF-NYINNGGGGNYINNGGYOKKAHOKKA HOKKA' will probably do the trick. Feel free to improvise if you get the urge.

It was a soggy evening. An aquatic circus of weeping.●(optional) By the end of it all, Queenie's dressing room was waist-deep in crumpled tissues.

When the three of them finally stopped crying, something strange happened. They looked around at the lake of tissues and, without quite knowing why, Hannah began to laugh. She laughed and laughed. Granny laughed and laughed. Queenie laughed and laughed.

Hannah laughed so hard, she fell off her chair, disappearing entirely under the surface of the tissue-lake, which made Queenie and Granny laugh even harder, until they realised that she might be lost down there and they reached out and hauled her up into the fresh air, still laughing, despite having several tissues stuck to her hair.

When they finally stopped laughing, Queenie

● Those of you with an interest in mucus will be pleased to hear that a large amount of snot was involved. Others, who find this kind of detail distasteful, may wish to skip this footnote, which, as you can see, is optional.

told Hannah that now they had the sad stuff out of
the way, it was time for some good news. 'I've saved
it until now,' she said, 'and it's a doozy. Your father's
here. At least, he's sort of here and sort of on his
way.'

'My father? You know who my father is?'

'Actually, no. I'm not entirely sure. It could be
Ernesto Espadrille or it could be Armitage Shank.
But the thing is, they're both here. Or will be.'

'Both of them!'

'Yes! Ernesto is on his way and Armitage is
already at the Oh, Wow! Centre. He's planning to
rob me tomorrow night. Isn't that wonderful!?'

'You like being robbed?'

'No, not that bit! The rest of it! Both of your
fathers will be here for tomorrow's show. And,
believe me, Armitage is not going to get away with
it, not unless he has the dastardliest scheme of his
entire dastardly, scheming life.'

'How do you know he doesn't have the dastardliest scheme of his entire dastardly, scheming life?'

'Well, maybe he does – but I can be just as dastardly as him, if not more so – and he will not get away with it, by the hairs on my chinny chin chin.'

'You don't have any hairs on your chinny chin chin. You're a woman.'

'It's just a turn of phrase, dear. And I do occasionally treat myself to the odd pluck.'

'So if Armitage is here,' said Hannah, 'does that mean Billy's here, too?'

'Yes! That's the whole point of the circus!'

'What do you mean?' asked Hannah, who was finding, yet again, that every answer to every question just seem to unfold more layers of puzzlement and confusion and seaweed and old trainers.

'Well – one of two points. I seem to have made myself bankrupt, which is kind of inconvenient. So the show is handy for that, because they're paying me a ton of money. But I also knew that if I came out of retirement, Armitage would appear and try to finish off his unfinished revenge. This whole thing is what they call a honeytrap. A lure. Because I knew that if he came, Billy would come. And I knew that if Billy came, and I timed it for Ernesto's release from prison, then I could help them find each other. I have a fan who works in the kitchens at Grimwood Scrubs, and he passed on a message to Ernesto explaining the plan. He's out of jail and he's on his way. He's coming to get Billy! I sent someone to tip off Billy, too, an old acquaintance of mine called Magwitch McDickens. He's a lovely chap – used to set the chess puzzles in my fanzine – but he can be a bit unreliable, so I'm not sure if the message got through.'

'Wowzer!' said Hannah. 'That's amazing! I'm so happy I think I might have to start crying again.'

'Don't!' said Granny. 'We've run out of tissues. What we need to do is find Billy. Tell him his father's coming. Tell him his granny's here. And his sister. That's a lot of news for a boy who thinks he's more or less an orphan.'

'Where is he?' said Hannah.

'He's here,' replied Queenie, confidently, before adding the word, 'somewhere,' not so confidently.

'How are we going to find him?'

'That's the only problem. I have no idea. But things have a habit of working out. So I suggest we go to bed now and start looking for him tomorrow.'

'Bed!?' said Hannah. 'How can you say that at a time like this? How could we possibly go to bed? Billy's here! We have to find him! We have to look! We have to tell him about Ernesto! We have to tell him about Granny! We have to tell him about me!

There's so much to do! We can't stop now! How could we go to bed? I'm not tired! I hate bed! Come on! Let's get going! *Bed?!* There's no way we can possibly . . .'

At this moment, Hannah's body began to topple. Quite soon, it finished toppling, landing softly on a mattress of only slightly snotty tissues. Her eyes were tight shut, and her breathing was deep and distant.

'She's asleep,' said Queenie to Granny, but there wasn't really much point in her saying this, because Granny was asleep, too, her false teeth rattling like a stick dragged over a cattle grid.

It had been a long day.

FOURTEEN

Apart but together

THAT NIGHT, CURLED INTO THE WARMTH of Narcissus, Billy dreamed a beautiful dream, of a woman on a trapeze. A woman who was like Queenie Bombazine, but wasn't Queenie Bombazine. A woman who was also like Hannah, but wasn't Hannah. She was beautiful and graceful and elegant, and she swung backwards and forwards through Billy's sleeping brain like some kind of angel, or blessing, or promise, or premonition, or something. Something good, anyway. More than good. Because though the dream woke him in the darkest, loneliest hour of the night, he woke with his heart feeling full and warm. He felt accompanied, protected and looked after, a feeling that for some of us is quite normal, but for Billy was rare and precious.

He closed his eyes again and tried to sleep, wanting to find his way back to that delicious dream, but dreams aren't like that. You can't chase them. Dreams find you, not the other way round, and this one had come and gone.

✳

Hannah woke at the same moment. She woke from what was possibly the exact same dream. A dream of a woman on a trapeze. A woman who was like Queenie Bombazine, but wasn't Queenie Bombazine. A woman who was also like Hannah, but wasn't Hannah. She was wearing a green rubber catsuit with a yellow lightning bolt streaking across the chest and down one leg. She was beautiful and graceful and elegant, and she swung backwards and forwards through Hannah's sleeping brain like some kind of angel, or blessing, or promise, or premonition, or something. Something good, anyway. More than good. Because though the dream woke her in the darkest, loneliest hour of the night, she woke with her heart feeling full and warm. She felt accompanied, protected and looked after, which was not a new sensation for Hannah, but on this occasion she had a strong sentiment that there was someone close by who was with her in that moment, right with her, not present in the same room, yet somehow closer than close.

FIFTEEN

Binary Tim's (not very) brilliant plan

THE NEXT MORNING, Hannah wake up in the presidential suite of the Oh, Wow! hotel. This was a room the size of a football pitch, except without any grass or goalposts. It was so big you could get lost in it, with a bed so wide you could get lost on your way from the middle to the edge, a sofa so plump you could get lost between the cushions, cupboards so enormous you could . . . I think you get the idea . . .

I seem to have got lost explaining how lost you

could get in this hotel room. Where was I again? What day is it? Who am I?

Oh, yes. I'm me and it's today and I was about to tell you how Queenie had carried Hannah up the night before, from her temporary bed of snotty tissues in the dressing room, and laid her down on the presidential four-poster, which was a significant improvement, luxury-wise.

Queenie had given Hannah a long lie-in, but she'd eventually been woken by the sound of Binary Tim, who was arriving for a breakfast meeting to discuss anti-Armitage security measures. Binary Tim was Queenie's IT 🎥 consultant and a specialist in high-tech anti-robbery surveillance. He wore strange glasses, which made his eyeballs look three times their actual size, not because of a particular problem with his eyesight, but because

---

🎥 If you see the word IT, that doesn't mean someone is shouting the word 'it' for no apparent reason. IT stands for Information Technology, which is a fancy term for computers. A more accurate term would be MAOTILUPTT, which stands for Mucking About On The Internet Looking Up Pointless Things Technology, but for some reason this acronym has never caught on.

he thought this would make him more alluring to women. In this, he was mistaken. Binary Tim had only a very sketchy knowledge of female psychology.

Hannah woke to hear Binary Tim outlining the scheme he had devised.

'We hook up a motion-sensor camera in the box office. I connect that to facial recognition software on my laptop, scan in an image of Armitage Shank, and, if someone with a Shank-like appearance enters, that will trigger a release mechanism on an ornamental medieval sword which I will install directly above the safe, which is where he's sure to be doing his dastardly deeds. This sword should do for him, but just in case he's in the wrong position when it falls, I can also connect the release mechanism to the office sprinkler system, causing that to be triggered at the same moment, except that I'll replace the water in the sprinkler tanks with an extremely powerful laxative fluid. This will cause Mr Shank to need the toilet with quite fabulous urgency, but he won't be aware that I have booby-trapped the nearest lavatory with a high-voltage electric current running through the toilet seat. I've also ordered some poisonous spiders on the internet which I have a feeling might come in handy as a fall-back option.'

'Hmmmm,' said Queenie, who didn't want to be discouraging, but who remained not entirely convinced by the plan. 'Do you think this might be a little overelaborate?'

'The sword doesn't have to be medieval. That's optional.'

'It's not just that. It's the whole thing.'

'What's wrong with it?'

'I don't want to cut his head off, I just want to stop him robbing me. I want to catch him in the act and get him sent to jail.'

'The sword can be blunt. Or we could use a

Viking club. That should just knock him out. And the electric current doesn't have to be fatal. Paralysis would be fine.'

'Why don't we just put in a camera to record what he does, and we can tip off security to arrest him on the way out.'

'That's all you want?'

'I think so.'

Binary Tim's three-times-normal-size eyeballs filled with three-times-normal-size tears. Big, wet golf balls of disappointment. 'You don't want the motion-triggered medieval sword?'

'I don't think we need that.'

'The electrified toilet seat?'

'I think that might be a hazard for the staff.'

'I could put an exploding cactus on the windowsill. Just in case.'

'That's very kind of you, but I think I'll pass on the exploding cactus.'

'Laxative in the sprinkler system?'

'Just water will be fine.'

'OK,' said Tim, looking more than a little crushed. 'If you're sure.'

'I'm sure.'

Queenie gave Binary Tim a kiss on the cheek by way of thank you, which seemed to cheer him up enormously, and he left in good spirits. It was only then that Queenie noticed Hannah was awake.

'Hannah, dear. You're up! What would you like for breakfast? Boiled egg, fried egg, poached egg, coddled egg, scrambled egg, devilled egg, eggs Benedict Cumberbatch or omelette? Or all of them. That's what I had and quite delicious it was, too.'

'What's eggs Benedict Cumberbatch?'

'It's poached egg on a muffin with bacon and hollandaise sauce served in a deerstalker hat. Delicious.'

'You like eggs, then?'

'Oh, yes. Absolutely. You can live off eggs and water and nothing else. Did you know that? Or maybe that was coconuts. Anyway, we can order you the whole egg medley and, if you don't finish it, I'll polish off your leftovers. Did you hear Binary Tim's plan?'

'Yes. He's very ambitious.'

'Wonderful man, but works best off a short rein. Wild imagination. Which is normally a good thing, but it's not what you want in an IT consultant.'

'So he's putting a camera in the box office?'

'That's the plan.'

'And that will catch Armitage?' asked Hannah.

'I think so.'

'But what about Billy? What if he's there, too? Will he get arrested?'

'We have to find him first. We have to warn him. If we want Armitage to meet his doooooooom, we have to make sure he commits the burglary, but without Billy taking part, and without Armitage noticing anything strange. It's a conundrum, and we need someone small and unobtrusive and cunning to get a message to Billy before the burglary takes place. Someone he knows and trusts who can sneak behind the lines of Armitage's operation without being noticed.'

'ME!✚ said Hannah.

'Yes,' replied Queenie. 'You. Now are you ready?'

'Of course I am.'

'Not before you've had your eggs you're not. Now eat up.'

Hannah ate up. The eggs Benedict Cumberbatch was the best breakfast she had ever tasted, though the deerstalker hat was a little chewy.

✚ ME stands for myalgic encephalomyelitis, which is a serious disease, though in this case it's just Hannah shouting the word 'me'. Acronyms can be awkward things, as anyone who works for the Paris Osteopathy Organisation will tell you.

SIXTEEN

Hannah on the rampage

HANNAH BOUNDED OUT of the presidential suite powered by a surge of egg-fuelled energy. Boy, she was buzzing.

Then she realised she had Queenie's alarm clock in her pocket. She switched it off and she stopped buzzing, which was a relief.

Hannah went down in the lift and up again, because she liked lifts, and down again, and out into the Oh, Wow! Centre, which was filled with excited people walking around, wondering why they were excited and how they had ended up in the middle of nowhere in a huge and pointless tent. They were there for the final night of Queenie Bombazine's Aquatic Circus, of course, but since it was just after breakfast time, these people had really arrived preposterously early, which perhaps explained their confusion.

Hannah went off to look for Billy. She hunted and hunted and hunted and hunted and hunted and hunted, but to no avail. He was nowhere to be found. Not even if you hunted and hunted and hunted and hunted and hunted and hunted.

Hannah's rampage was not going to plan. In fact, it was proving a little monotonous.

She was so disappointed that she decided to console herself with a stick of candy floss.

Yes! Candy floss!

From the candy floss stall!

Which is when she found him!

Oh, joy!

Oh, rapture!

Oh, bliss!

Oh, stop using exclamation marks!

I can't help it!

Stop!

I can't!

You have to!

I'll try!

The reason why Hannah had been unable to find Billy was because he'd spent the entire morning on the roof of the candy floss stall waiting for Hannah, and the roof of the candy floss stall was a place Hannah had not thought to include in her hunt.

No sooner had Hannah ordered her candy floss than Billy leapt down from his perch to give her an enormous hug-of-the-century. Unfortunately, in his enthusiasm, Billy failed to notice that his ankles

were tangled in a string of bunting. So his top half leapt down, but his legs didn't. This happened just as Hannah was passed her stick of candy floss.

The upshot of this simultaneous candy floss delivery and bunting entanglement was that just as Hannah was about to take her first bite, an unidentifiable head plunged down and hung there, buried inside the cloud of pink sugar.

Hannah's first thought was

that she was being attacked by a cunning, airborne candy floss thief. When she heard the word 'Help!' emerging from inside her candy floss, she began to think maybe this person wasn't a thief, but she still couldn't understand why they would choose to dangle inside her mid-morning snack.

'Hannah!' said the candy floss. 'It's me!'

'Who?' said Hannah to the candy floss.

'ME!' replied the candy floss aka Billy, who wasn't thinking straight at this moment, on account of being upside down, tangled up in bunting, suffocating inside a portion of novelty fairground food.

Hannah decided the best thing to do was to take a large bite of the floss. This bite revealed to her the most joyous and wonderful sight she had ever seen. Billy! Swathed in what now looked like a fluffy pink balaclava.

'Bmmmmmlmmmmmmmmm!' yelled Hannah,

whose mouth was too full for any successful attempt at speech.

'Hannah!' said Billy. 'I've been looking for you everywhere!'

'I've been looking for *you* everywhere,' replied Hannah. 'I never thought I'd find you here. Inside my snack. How did you do that?'

'Magic,' said Billy, modestly. (Every skilled performer develops an instinct for making mistakes look like part of the show.)

'I'm so pleased we found each other,' gabbled Hannah. 'I've got amazing things to tell you. It turns out you're my brother! Or my half-brother! Depending on who my father is! Which I don't know just yet, but both of the men who might be are going to be here tonight which means I might be about to find out. And one of them's your father. He's on his way! He's coming to find you! And either way we're definitely siblings. Isn't that just the best thing ever!'

'It really is! I can't believe it!' said Billy, who was so delighted by this news that he completely forgot he was hanging by the ankles from a string of bunting.

Nature, however, has a way of curing people of this kind of forgetfulness. Billy's reminder of the unusual circumstances surrounding his reunion with his sister came about only a second or two later, at the moment when the bunting tore, releasing him to the unforgiving mercies of gravity.

Gravity, like other laws of physics, has little truck with sentiment.

Billy crashed downwards, landing on top of Hannah, giving her that hug he'd been meaning to give only a short while earlier, though as it turned out this wasn't so much an I'm-so-pleased-to-see-you hug as the more unusual terribly-sorry-but-I-seem-to-be-using-you-as-a-landing-mat variety.

Hannah didn't mind. She was far too happy to

let a small matter like being knocked over and landed on bother her.

When they'd finally untangled themselves from one another, Hannah suddenly spoke in a sharp whisper. 'Quick! We have to hide!'

'From who?'

'Armitage! We've made plan! Me and Queenie and Granny! Actually, Granny isn't a huge part of it since she keeps dozing off, but there is a plan! Armitage can't see us together! Because tonight he's finally going to meet his *dooooooooooooom!*'

SEVENTEEN

The golden phablet

ARMITAGE SHANK WAS IN A BAD MOOD.
Yeah, yeah, what else is new? Armitage was always in a bad mood.

These things are relative, so when I said Armitage was in a bad mood, I meant he was in a mood measured on his special scale of badness, on which good is bad, and bad is just appallingly, atrociously, unimaginably, stinkily grumpy. That's the mood we were talking about. Imagine if you had one foot stuck in a mousetrap, the other in a box of snakes, were wearing clothes made of sandpaper, had just accidentally dyed your hair luminous purple, and a bag of rotten haddock had just been tied to your nose by someone who was also tickling the back of your neck with soggy pondweed. Imagine what kind of mood that would put you in. That's how Armitage felt. Not because he was in the unpleasant situation I have just described, but because he had lost his phone, and he hated losing his phone.

The thing is – and Armitage didn't know this – he hadn't lost his phone. His phone had been stolen (or, rather, borrowed) by Billy. If Armitage had known this, Billy would have been in a whole huge bucket of trouble, but – IRONY ALERT – Billy had learned exceptionally good thieving skills from Armitage, so had little trouble taking his phone without raising the alarm.

'I need to send out a jeet on Jitter saying that

I've lost my phone, but I can't because I'VE LOST MY PHONE!' yelled Armitage, who, having searched everywhere in vain, was now lying on the floor, sobbing, beating the ground with his fists. Armitage suffered from a really rather undignified tendency to indulge his moods.♟

'I'm sure it will turn up,' replied Billy, who at that moment realised he had forgotten to turn the phone off and, since it was in his pocket,

♟ Personally, I blame his mother. She was too hard on him as a child. Or too soft on him. One of the two. Or maybe both. But that's another story. Suffice to say, any woman who lavishes more love on her collection of pet newts than on her son is unlikely to rear a happy child. (The newts turned out great, though. Pillars of society, they are.)

an incoming phone call would give him away. Armitage had no friends, so this was unlikely, but nonetheless, Billy decided he had to get out of there fast.

'I have to get out of here fast,' said Billy.

'Why?' sobbed Armitage, who was now beating his chest with one hand and pulling a fistful of hair with the other, while glancing at himself in the mirror to gauge which action had a more tragic appearance.

'I . . . er . . . fancy a bit of candy floss.'

'Good idea. Get me one, too,' said Armitage, suddenly leaping towards Billy and eyeballing him with an intense stare. 'You mustn't be too discouraged by what has happened today. I know it's hard. I know our rampage may seem doomed and cursed right now, but we have to remember what is within reach. After tonight, we can use Queenie's money to buy whatever phone we want.

I might even get you one. In fact, if our plan comes off, tomorrow I was going to go out first thing and buy THIS!'

Armitage reached into a pocket of his safari suit, and was annoyed to find the climax to his masterpiece of motivational speaking ruined by the fact that the 'THIS!' in question was not there.

He looked in another pocket, then another one. Then another one.

Armitage's safari suit, designed for rampages of a long, complex and gadget-heavy nature, had seventy-three pockets. It was in the seventy-first pocket that Armitage eventually found what he was looking for.

'THIS!' he repeated, triumphantly pulling out a tightly folded piece of paper, though even Armitage had to admit the gesture would have been more dramatic had he tried this pocket seventy pockets earlier.

He handed the paper to Billy. It was a picture of a sock, torn from a magazine.

'A sock?'

'No, the other side.'

Billy turned over the paper. 'A phone?'

'No!' replied Armitage. 'A phablet. The pinnacle of human technological achievement. The ultimate communication device in the entire history of the human race. The perfect union of smartphone and tablet computer. The iSung Gooseberry 7d special edition, with fingerprint recognition, iris recognition, recognition recognition and recognition recognition recognition. The gadget of our dreams.'

Billy, who did not have gadgets in his dreams, looked a little nonplussed.☺ 'What's recognition recognition recognition?' he asked.

'It's like recognition recognition, but faster. It's a whole new generation of recognition. I've been

---

☺ It is not possible to look plussed. Only nonplussed. Most people, when they look nonplussed, also look inert, which is interesting, because it is also not possible to look ert. At least I've never managed it.

reading about it in *What Phablet?* for months. Jitter has been alight with rumours, and now it's on the market! We can be almost the first!'

'Oh,' said Billy. 'That's . . . great.'

Armitage held Billy firmly with one hand on each shoulder and gave him an encouraging squeeze. 'There is hope, Billy. We just have to put adversity behind us and march on bravely, undeterred by the curses that fate tosses into our path!'

'OK,' said Billy. 'I'll try.'

'One day we'll have every gadget a person could possibly want! I promise you! At least, I will, but I'll let you borrow them sometimes, if you're good, especially the obsolete ones.'

'Thanks. I can hardly wait.'

'You don't have to. The waiting's almost over, Billy. The future is about to arrive.'

'Isn't the future always about to arrive?'

Armitage thought for a moment. 'It is. You're right. But not this future. Not a future as high-spec and brand new and gadgety as the one we're going to have. Everything we've been deprived of all these years is about to fall into our lap. It's not easy being a thief. It's a very uncertain career, with poor promotion prospects, a high drop-out rate and no pension plan. We've waited a long time for our moment of triumph, Billy, but tonight's the night!'

'Great. I'm going to pop out for that candy floss.'

'There seems to be an awful lot of candy floss stuck in your hair. Why can't you just eat that?'

'Er . . . it's gone off. Look.'

Billy plucked a lump from out of his fringe and handed it to Armitage, who stared suspiciously at the pink dollop, which looked chewier and hairier than candy floss ought to. In fact, it looked more like a skinned rodent than a fairground treat.

'OK,' said Armitage. 'Off you go. But make sure

you're back in good time for our dastardly plan.'

'I will be. Don't worry,' said Billy, though inside his inner cackle was having a secret, silent cackle-party. The future really was about to arrive and not the one Armitage wanted.

EIGHTEEN

The secret rendezvous

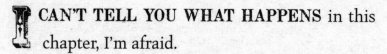

I CAN'T TELL YOU WHAT HAPPENS in this chapter, I'm afraid.

Why not?

Because it's a secret, *obviously*. If I told you, it would just be a normal rendezvous. All I can tell you is this. Billy snuck out. Or is it sneaked out? Or should that be snicked out? Snucked? Snacked? Whatever – he left in a sly and secretive fashion and met up with Hannah in a secret place.

Where?

I can't tell you. Obviously!

They had a short meeting, during which they perfected their plan to foil Armitage's plan, hugged a little more, chatted about Important Things, and picked the last of the dried candy floss out of Billy's hair (which proved to be a much more enjoyable activity than you would have thought).

Billy also handed over Armitage's phone to Hannah, as arranged.

Hannah reminded Billy that his father could be arriving any minute, which wasn't strictly necessary, since Billy had spent the last two days thinking about little else.

Billy reminded Hannah that the father who might be arriving any minute might also be her father. This was a pointless statement for exactly the same reason.

Parting is such sweet sorrow, wrote an old bloke in a puffy shirt many, many years ago, and he was

---

Grooming is an important form of social bonding for all primates, including humans. If people spent more time picking things out of other people's hair, we'd all get on a lot better. We really would. If the United Nations began each session with a spot of international grooming, the planet would be a far more peaceful place. But that's enough about world peace. We've got more important things to deal with.

right. He wasn't talking about hairstyles, either. He was talking about saying goodbye to someone you don't want to say goodbye to, and that's exactly what it was like for Billy and Hannah. But they had to separate one last time, in order to enact their fiendishly clever plan.

Good old Billy and Hannah, eh? Aren't they wonderful and brave and clever and resourceful and kind and good at picking stuff out of each other's hair? One day, somebody should write a book about them.

They have? Who? When? Where can I buy it? Does it have pictures?

NINETEEN
The dastardly plan meets the anti-dastardly-plan plan

THAT NIGHT, Qeenie's final performance at the Oh, Wow! Centre was truly spectacular. Of course, Queenie Bombazine's shows were always spectacular, but this one was extra spectacularly spectacular.

Every time you watch a movie, it's the same, but when it comes to live performance, no two nights are identical. Every audience is different, and each audience is an ingredient in what happens on the stage. Performers can feel when the audience is interested, excited, tense, scared, bored, sleepy, restless, alert, thrilled to the point of heart attack, or asleep. Nobody knows how this happens, you can just feel it, and every performer in every kind of performance adjusts the pace of what they are doing to fit with the response of the spectators.

Sometimes, something special happens. The performance and the response gel, to produce a perfect show. Every laugh, sigh and gasp comes exactly when the performer knows it is going to come, and even a perfectly rehearsed, slick-as-clockwork show lifts to another level. All actors hold nights like this dear in their hearts, and they only come once in a while. When they are gone, you have to just let them go. Like dreams, and escaped budgerigars, you can't chase after them and get them back. Even if you try and do everything identically the following night, it won't be the same.

Queenie's closing night at the Oh, Wow! was one of those nights. Every single person there was rapt for the entire show.◾

Everyone, I should say, apart from two people at the back, who, when the inflatable palm trees for Reginald Clench's tuba-playing Hawaiian maiden routine appeared, slipped out of the arena and headed for the box office, tiptoeing in a distinctly dastardly fashion.

Those two people, of course, were Armitage Shank and his unfortunate adopted son, heir to the Shank Entertainment Empire, Billy.

Which brings us to a third un-rapt, or perhaps I should say differently-rapt, member of the audience: a girl in the front row, who had her opera glasses trained not on the stage, but in the other direction entirely, towards the two dastardly tiptoers.

Where they went, she followed.

◾ That's rapt, not wrapped. If you ever find yourself thinking that learning to spell is a boring waste of time, remember this as an example of the confusion that can be caused by clumsy spilling.

To where did Armitage and Billy (and Hannah) tiptoe?

To a pillar. A large pillar holding up the roof of the Oh, Wow!

Why? Had Armitage suddenly taken an interest in the wonders of modern engineering? Was he thinking of building his own huge and pointless tent in the middle of somewhere else?

Oh, no. This pillar had been chosen for three purely practical reasons. Firstly, because it was large enough to hide behind; secondly, because it overlooked the box office; and thirdly, there is no thirdly, I just counted wrong.

Armitage stared at the box office door in the way a cat stares at a mouse hole. I'm not saying he went down on all fours and purred, I am simply trying to point out the intense fixity of his gaze, combined with an undertone of menace and greed.

Oh, Armitage, why are you so mean? Why do

you steal? Why do you covet other people's money just so you can buy more stuff that you don't even really need?**?**

Within a minute, Reginald Clench walked out of the box office, carrying a tuba, dressed in his stage costume of yellow flip-flops, grass skirt and a garland of jasmine flowers around his neck. In fact, his gait was closer to a skip than a walk, such was Clench's excitement as he headed towards the stage. Not so long ago, his tuba-playing, Hawaiian maiden routine had been a mere hobby; now he was performing to a live audience in the country's largest auditorium. Nothing had ever made him quite so proud and happy, not even Rudolph's first march.

'You stay here!' hissed Armitage to Billy. 'If anyone comes, give the signal to bail out. Three sharp whistles. OK?'

'OK.'

? These are rhetorical questions, which means they don't have an answer. Or if they do have an answer, nobody cares what it is. Why, oh why do people ask rhetorical questions? What is the point? Does anyone know? Does anyone care? What am I talking about?

'Keep your eyes peeled.'

'I will.'

'This is it, Billy. Untold riches! More phablets than in your wildest dreams!'

'That's hard to imagine.'

'I'm telling you, one of these days they're going to award me the Nobel Prize for Evil.'

'I don't think there is a Nobel Prize for Evil,' replied Billy.

'There will be. Mark my words.'

Leering his leeriest leer, Armitage scurried away to commence what he was confident would be the most dramatic and lucrative burglary of his entire burglarising career.

Reginald had locked the door of the box office, of course, but Armitage could pick locks as easily as he could pick his nose. In fact, if he felt like showing off, he could do both at once, one with each hand. But this was no occasion for fancy routines. He broke through the box office door as quickly as he could and slipped in.

Like all good burglarisers, he had thought in advance about the countermeasures that might have been put in place by way of security, and no sooner was he through the door than he stood dead still, scouring the room with his beady, nasty, mean, piggy⤙ eyes.

Queenie was no fool. Armitage knew a trap would have been laid for him. But what was it, and where would he find it, and how would he get round it?

✳

As we have already seen, Armitage had a lookout in place. But this lookout was not looking out. He was waving happily at Hannah, who had appeared from the auditorium just as Armitage disappeared into the box office.

Now that Hannah was there, with Armitage

⤙ This adjective is not intended to give offence to any porcine readers. Some pigs have lovely, intelligent eyes, and charming personalities. But, let's face it, personal hygiene is rarely a strong point.

right in the middle of his burglary, the task was simple. She had to call the police, on Armitage's phone, but not before Billy had time to run off and hide. Because, whether he liked it or not, Billy was an accomplice. And, however wonderful it would be for Armitage to meet his doooooom, it would all be for nothing if Billy met his dooooooom with him.

The plan was already planned. They didn't even need to exchange a single word. Hannah looked at Billy; Billy looked at Hannah; they nodded; Billy handed over the phone and ran off to his secret hiding place.

Hannah counted to a hundred, dialled 999, and told the police that if they came to the box office of the Oh, Wow! Centre as quickly as possible, they would catch the country's most notorious burglariser in the act of an audacious crime. She also told them that she could hand over the

burglariser's phone, which was bound to contain
evidence of his dastardly, dismal, detestable, dire,
disgraceful, deceitful, devious, dubious, despicable,
dirty, depraved, dishonest, disgusting, dreadful
deeds.

But, only a second after she hung up, something
extraordinary happened – something that had no
place whatsoever in Hannah and Billy's anti-
dastardly-plan plan.

A man appeared. A man in
a hurry. A man still dressed
in prison uniform.

Hannah had seen the
old posters. She recognised
him immediately. This was
Ernesto Espadrille.

The shock of it froze
her to the spot and
seemed to glue her

mouth shut. She wanted to run towards him and throw herself into his arms, she wanted to shout to him that they simply had to talk, she wanted to call out and tell him where to find Billy, but before she had a chance to do any of these things, Ernesto slipped away, following Armitage into the box office.

Hannah couldn't just stand there and watch. She had to speak to him. So, in a sudden and major departure from the plan she had made with Billy, she ran towards the box office after Armitage and Ernesto, her two maybe-fathers.

In a calmer frame of mind, Hannah might have sensed that the middle of a burglary, with the police already on the way, was possibly not the best time to resolve the question of her paternity, but Hannah was not in a remotely calm frame of mind whatsoever. The conundrum at the very heart of her identity wasn't a topic she could put aside and forget about, not for a moment.

This was a one-off opportunity. Both maybe-fathers were in the same place! That was never going to happen again. One of them had just got out of jail and the other one was almost certainly about to go to jail. This presented a very small window of opportunity – a fleeting chance to confront them both. So what if they were busy? So what if the police were coming? So what if just being in that room put you in danger of immediate arrest? Hannah *had* to know which father was which and who was who and what was what. She couldn't wait a moment longer. Granny's confusing, long-winded, Russian-doll tales just weren't good enough. Hannah needed the truth, and this was her chance to go and get it.

So off she went, without even pausing to fear for the consequences.

Fearlessness is an admirable attribute.

Sometimes. Other times, not so much.

✳

At this point, with things getting a little complicated, we have to step back a few moments in time. Don't worry, we aren't going anywhere seaweedy or old-trainery. We're just skipping back one fragrant little time-hiccup to the moment we last saw Armitage.

He has just stepped into the box office. He is standing dead still, scouring the room for security devices. His skilled eye soon falls on a suspicious-looking item. Of course, in this room, at this moment, Armitage himself was the most suspicious-looking item, what with him being a burglar in the middle of a burglary, but we are inside Armitage's head now and, through his eyes, suspicious-looking items were items whose purpose was to stop burglaries. Yes, folks, this is what it feels like to be inside the warped, topsy-turvy brain of a master criminal. Weird, isn't it?

The object that caught his eye was an award. A suspiciously shiny, new-looking award. A trophy, in fact, awarding Bean-Counting Functionary of the Month status to Arthur Tariff in the discounts, supplements and rip-offs department. What made this trophy suspicious was the fact that it had a wire snaking out from the back, and a small hole in the front, through which was visible a tiny lens. Armitage knew immediately what this was: a security camera, a disguised security camera, put in place for the purpose of catching him.

Armitage reached into the twenty-third largest pocket of his safari suit and took out a piece of thick card. Onto this card he wrote: *Ha ha ha HA HA HA HA HA ha ha ha ha ha ha HA! HA! HA! HA! TOO OBVIOUS!*

He stuck this piece of card in front of the lens of the camera, ensuring that all it would record was his cackle and gloat. And oh, how Armitage loved to cackle and gloat. If anyone ever asked him if he had any hobbies, this was the answer he usually gave: cackling and gloating. And badminton.

Now the burglarising could begin.

Except for . . . goodness me . . . what on earth was that?! A statue? Or a dog?

Armitage had just spotted Rudolph. Rudolph was standing to attention. Motionless. He was upright, in a kennel especially designed for upright dogs, twice the height, with an arched opening right to the top. It looked more like a sentry box than a kennel. In fact, it was a sentry box. Rudolph was on guard duty. Just like the soldiers outside Buckingham Palace, his body was rigid and unmoving.

Armitage stared at Rudolph. Rudolph stared dead ahead.

If this was a guard dog it didn't seem to be

doing a very good job.

On other burglarising missions, Armitage took with him a raw steak, for the purpose of distracting guard dogs, but he hadn't been expecting to find a dog in the box office, so this time he was steakless. He patted through the pockets of his safari suit, and in the twenty-seventh one on the left he found a square of chocolate that he'd stolen from Billy earlier in the day.

'Here you go, boy,' he said, putting it gingerly at the dog's feet.

The dog still didn't move.

'You're a weird dog,' said Armitage.

You're a weird man, thought Rudolph, but he didn't bark or twitch.

Armitage concluded that this was either the world's worst guard dog, or that it was actually dead and stuffed. What he didn't even consider was that Rudolph might have been instructed to observe, but not to intervene until a particular trigger point had been reached.

Armitage now turned his attention to the safe. Joy of joys, wonder of wonders, rapture of raptures, the thing wasn't even locked! Distracted by the excitement of getting changed into his Hawaiian maiden costume, Clench had been slack. He'd made a catastrophic error.

Of all the things to forget!

Armitage let out his biggest cackle of the day as he reached in and began to stuff his pockets with money. He would have quite liked to include 'stuffing my pockets with money' on his list of hobbies, but to be honest this didn't really happen often enough for Armitage to count it as anything more than an occasional pastime.

Just as Armitage was beginning to think this was the easiest burglary of his entire career, he heard a voice in the room behind him, a voice he

dimly, distantly recognised from his dim and distant past.

'ARMITAGE SHANK! WHAT ON EARTH ARE YOU DOING? IN FACT, I KNOW EXACTLY WHAT YOU ARE DOING AND I'M NOT EVEN SLIGHTLY SURPRISED. NOW WHERE'S MY SON?'

Armitage spun round and gazed up in horror. The voice belonged to a man he had not seen for many years. A man he thought was safely locked up in jail. A man in the top ten on Armitage's list of People Who Will Want To Do Me In If They Ever Find Me Again. Ernesto Espadrille.

TWENTY

Two angry men, one brave girl and a massive heap of cash

HAD HE BEEN THINKING MORE CLEARLY, Armitage might have concentrated on finishing stuffing his pockets with money; he might even have tried to ignore Ernesto's surprising outburst; but the idea of Billy not being his son was one that made Armitage's brain sizzle with uncontainable fury.

'*Your* son?' snapped Armitage, his moustache quivering like a plucked harp string. 'You don't have a son!'

'Don't give me that nonsense,' replied Ernesto. 'Just tell me where to find Billy!'

'I tell you, he's not your son, he's mine. You ran off and abandoned him years ago. He can't ever forgive you for that. Luckily, I was around to pick up the pieces, or who knows what would have happened to him? Disappointment, debility, destruction, distress, despair, defeat and destitution. He calls me father now, and has completely forgotten that anyone else has any claim on him. If he sees you, and remembers what you did to him, it'll break his heart.'

Ernesto's response to these words was to shrink. A human being cannot literally diminish in size from one moment to the next, but that is exactly what appeared to happen to Ernesto. The pain of hearing these words seemed to knock the life out of him. Within the few seconds it took Armitage to utter this speech, Ernesto gave the appearance of shrivelling into a smaller, lesser man.

'I . . . I . . . didn't abandon him,' stammered Ernesto. 'I had no choice.'

'Billy knows you betrayed him. He loathes you. I've tried my best to teach him not to hate – to have a kind and gentle soul – but the pain runs too deep. You have scarred him to the very bones.'

'I . . . I . . . came for him as soon as I could.'

'Too late. Many, many years too late. Now go away and leave me to finish my work before you wound him any further.'

Suddenly, a voice piped up from the doorway. The voice of a young girl. A voice supercharged with outrage and anger and also a little bit of loveliness.

'LIES!' bellowed Hannah. 'IT'S ALL LIES! DON'T BELIEVE A WORD HE SAYS!'

'Who are you?' said Ernesto.

'That's what I came here to ask you,' replied

Hannah. 'Who *am* I? You two are the only people who know the answer.'

'Oh, my dizzy uncle!' yelped Armitage. 'It's *you!* You're that girl! The one who tricked Billy! The one who stole all the things I had stolen and gave them back! How did you get here? Who *are* you? Who are you working for? Why won't you leave me alone?'

The sight of this mysterious, theft-foiling girl gave Armitage a cold, porridgey feeling in the pit of his stomach. Last time, she had been Very Bad News Indeed. He did not want her there. Not one little bit.

Hannah had no interest in any of Armitage's questions. She leapt towards Ernesto and grabbed his hands in hers, looking up passionately into his eyes. 'Everything Armitage just said is a lie! Billy loves you! He knows you didn't abandon him! He thinks about you every day! Armitage forces him to steal and do bad things and he doesn't want to do any of them! He wants to be with you. He's been waiting and waiting for you to come back and get him and as soon as he sees you he'll be the happiest boy in the world and he won't ever want to see Armitage for a single second ever again, because Armitage is a bad, bad, bad person and you're not and Billy wants to be with you again more than anything else in the whole world including chocolate.'

'Chocolate?' said Ernesto and Armitage together.

'Maybe that last bit about chocolate doesn't make any sense. The point is, everything Armitage just said is a lie. Billy knows he's your son. And I think I am, too! Not your son, I mean your daughter. Am I? You have to tell me, because, if it's not you, it's him!' said Hannah, jabbing a finger towards Armitage. 'And frankly I'd rather have a warthog for a father than that horrible, rotten, lying thief.'

'Daughter?' said Ernesto and Armitage together.

'My mother was Esmeralda Espadrille. I was born exactly twelve years ago yesterday while she was on a world tour. My granny says there are two people who could be my father. You or you. I *have* to know. And it *has* to be you, Ernesto. Please, please, please tell me you're my father.'

At this moment, two strange things happened. The first one was hardly surprising, given Hannah's phone call. It was the sudden interruption of a police siren.

The second thing, far stranger, was Armitage's reaction to this sound. As if suddenly overwhelmed by a wave of inexplicable and uncharacteristic generosity, he leapt forward and began to pull all the money out of his pockets and shove it into the pockets of Ernesto's prison uniform. (Such was Ernesto's hurry to see his son again that he hadn't paused to change out of his prison clothes into something a little less suspicious. This, as we are shortly to discover, was a costly error.)

As the sound of police boots approached, Armitage bent over and thrust his head into Ernesto's armpit, grabbing Ernesto's arm and squeezing it around his own throat.

'Help! Help!' yelled Armitage. 'He's got me! Please don't shoot! I'm a hostage! He's got me round the neck and he's going to throttle me unless he gets all this money. I'm so scared! He's a monster.'

'What are you talking about?' said Ernesto, trying to pull away, but he couldn't, because Armitage had his arm gripped firmly in strangling position. Meanwhile, the rest of Armitage's body was writhing as if he was struggling to get free.

'Ow!' said Armitage. 'Please help me! I'm terrified!'

'Freeze!' shouted a firm, policemanny voice. 'Put your arms up.'

Armitage let go of Ernesto and crumpled,

choking, onto the floor. Ernesto raised his arms, but only for a moment, because the policeman immediately pushed him against a wall and clamped him into handcuffs.

'Wait!' yelled Hannah. 'It's all lies! Armitage is the thief.'

'She's his accomplice,' said Armitage, in a hoarse, just-strangled voice. 'She's his daughter and she wants to get him off.'

'I'm his daughter! Am I really? Or are you just saying that to get me into trouble?'

'She doesn't even know who she is!' said Armitage to the policeman. 'The pair of them are criminally insane. They should be locked up forever.'

'I haven't done anything!' said Ernesto. 'I'm just looking for my son.'

'And he can't even keep track of his own children,' said Armitage. 'He's a bad parent on top of everything else.'

'I'm not a thief!' protested Ernesto, as the policeman began to pull him away.

'Very convincing,' said the policeman, sarcastically. 'Your pockets are stuffed with money from an open safe, you've been holding a hostage at strangulation point and you're already wearing prison uniform. I'd say this is an open and shut case.'

'I haven't done anything!' said Ernesto.

'He hasn't done anything!' said Hannah.

'*Woof!*' said Rudolph, in agreement.

'Oh, my neck!' said Armitage. 'The pain is

indescribable! I feel like I've swallowed a chainsaw! I think I need a breathing tube. Call an ambulance.'

Suddenly, there was a very loud crash, as a trapeze, dangling from who knows where, smacked into the side of the box office, sending Queenie Bombazine in full Mermaid of the Skies costume through the window. Shards of glass flew everywhere, but Queenie appeared unharmed.

'That man hasn't done anything!' she bellowed. 'It's my money and he can have as much of it as he wants. No crime has been committed here, except for by this slimeball – Armitage Shank – who is wanted by every police force in the country.'

Everyone was rather taken aback by this spectacular entrance, so much so that a long silence filled the room.

The policeman, who was a big circus fan, and was at this moment feeling distinctly star-struck, responded in a rather unprofessional manner. He gave Queenie a round of applause. His name, incidentally, was Bill, but since we already have a boy called Billy in this story, to avoid confusion the policeman shall henceforth be known as Old Bill.

'Well?' said Queenie, fighting the instinct to take a bow. 'Let him go!'

'I'm afraid I can't do that,' replied Old Bill, suddenly remembering that he was on duty. 'Robbery is robbery is robbery, even if the victim of the robbery subsequently claims in suspicious circumstances that she wanted to be robbed in the first place. He's guilty as sin, madam, and it's my job to enforce the law. In fact, if you weren't well known as a fine and upstanding citizen, I'd have a good mind to arrest you as an accomplice in the crime of burgling yourself, but instead I think I'll just ask for your autograph.'

'Burgling myself!? What utter nonsense!'

'I saw them whispering to each other earlier,' Armitage mock-whispered to Old Bill. 'Plotting. They're definitely in it together, along with that girl over there. She's the worst.'

'If you could just sign this bit of paper here,' said the policeman, ignoring Armitage, 'and write, "For Glenda. Best of luck with the hip replacement." It's my wife. She's a huge fan.'

'I don't care how much of a fan she is and how many hips she's having replaced! You may not have my autograph! Unless you release this man – in which case I will sign anything you like as many times as you like.'

Old Bill pondered for a moment, then sadly

shook his head. 'Sorry, madam, that's more than my job's worth. But I want you to know I'm your biggest fan. Me and Glenda. Joint biggest. We buy tickets to all your shows. Except tonight, obviously, because I'm working. And what with Glenda's hip and everything that was another problem. But usually—'

'You're my stupidest fan is what you are.'

'That's very rude,' replied Old Bill. 'You're a very rude lady. Glenda will be so disappointed to hear what you're really like.'

'You're arresting the wrong man! You are taking away an innocent, decent citizen and leaving behind the burglarising scourge of the nation!'

'That's as may be,' said Old Bill, 'but there's no call for bad manners. Now goodbye, madam, and no hard feelings.'

'Yes hard feelings. Very hard feelings indeed! Rock hard!'

'This is all going to be very hard to explain to Glenda,' said Old Bill, sadly, as he dragged Ernesto away.

'I'm innocent!' yelled Ernesto. 'That man's framed me!'

'He's guilty!' yelled Armitage. 'He tried to frame *me!*'

'He's innocent!' yelled Hannah.

'Guilty!' yelled Armitage.

'Innocent!' yelled Hannah.

'Guiltly guilty guilty!' yelled Armitage.

'Innocent innocent innocent times a hundred no returns!' yelled Hannah.

'Guilty times infinity, so there!' yelled Armitage.

'You're very immature,' said Hannah.

'*You're* very immature,' said Armitage.

'Innocent times infinity plus one!' yelled Hannah.

'Guilty times guilty times infinity plus infinity!' yelled Armitage.

'There's no such thing as infinity plus infinity, because infinity is already infinity!' yelled Hannah.

'Yes there is!' yelled Armitage.

Perhaps we should leave this debate on the finer points of criminal justice and mathematics here. You get the gist.

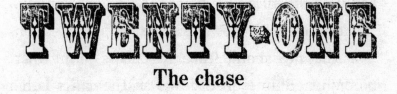

TWENTY-ONE

The chase

While Hannah and Armitage discussed the nature of infinity, Billy gazed down anxiously at the atrium from his secret, high-up hiding place. Was Armitage about to meet his doom? Had the police caught him with his hands in the safe? Would Ernesto swoop in at the perfect moment and take Billy away to a life of endless circussy wonderfulness? Or would Armitage sneak out of trouble again and walk away with the phablet of his dreams?

These were the questions pounding round Billy's head while he waited. And as we know – but he doesn't – the answers to these four questions were no, no, no and probably.

When Billy looked down and saw his father being dragged away in handcuffs, his heart very nearly broke.

'Dad!' he called, leaning out from his balcony high above the atrium. 'Dad! Is that you!? What's happening? Why are you in handcuffs?'

Ernesto stopped and looked around frantically, desperate to catch a glimpse of his son, but he couldn't see Billy anywhere.

'Up here! I'm up here!'

'Billy? Is that you?'

Billy was waving furiously, outside the nick-nack, bric-a-brac, tic-tac, pack-a-mac, quick-snack, backpack and roof-rack shop, so far up that Ernesto could barely see him. Billy knew that if he tried to run down the stairs or use a lift, his father would be gone before he could reach him. He did a swift calculation on the topic of angles, trajectories and the solidity of candy-floss stall roofs, then launched himself off the balcony into mid-air.

'Billlllllyyyyyyyyyy!' wailed Ernesto, thinking he had fallen, terrified that the tragedy of Esmeralda's death might be repeating itself in front of his eyes.

'Daaaaaaaaaaaaaaaaaaaad!' shouted Billy, as he did a back somersault with a double pike and triple flip-flop and quadruple wing-ding.

This was Esmeralda's signature move. Ernesto had never seen anyone else do it. Until now. And he had certainly never seen anyone do it as part of a perfect descent onto the canvas roof of a candy-floss stall, leading to a neat trampoline bounce, a couple more somersaults, and an immaculate landing.

'BILLY!' said Ernesto, his eyes filling with tears.

'Dad! I've been waiting for you,' replied Billy, throwing himself into his father's arm or, rather, into the place where Ernesto's arms would have been if they weren't handcuffed behind his back.

Imagine that! Your long-lost son! A tender, yearned-for embrace! Handcuffs! Oh, pass me a tissue. No, more than that – I need a whole box. Actually, make it two boxes and a towel. And a mop.

Old Bill was so moved by this handcuff-hug that his eyes were now brimming with tears as well. 'I…I…I'm sorry,' he sobbed, 'but the hugging of suspects is . . . is against regulations. I . . . I . . . boohoo . . . sniffle sniffle ♦ . . . I'm going to have to insist on the immediate termination of . . . of . . . oh, it's hard being a policeman. You have to be so mean sometimes, and I'm not a mean person. I like sunshine and flowers and balloons and kittens,

♦ It is highly unusual to say the word 'sniffle' instead of actually sniffling. Old Bill was wellknown throughout the Middle of Nowhere regional force as an eccentric weeper and unorthodox sniffler.

especially fluffy tabby ones with white paws and cute little pink noses ... Where were we again ...? Er ...'

'*WOOF*!' barked Rudolph.

But everyone ignored him. There was far too much going on for anyone to pay any attention to a mere dog. Even one who could stand like a meerkat.

'*WOOF WOOF*!' barked Rudolph again, dismayed, as he often was, by the idiocy, blindness, scruffiness, unpunctuality and bad posture of the human race.

'NOBODY MOVE!' boomed a voice from up in the atrium. 'HE'S GETTING AWAY!' This was the voice of an old lady, but an old lady in possession of an unusually powerful pair of lungs. Everybody looked up. The owner of the voice was so far away that for a moment she was unrecognisable. Then, without any warning, she launched herself off the balcony, performing a back somersault with a double pike, triple flip-flop and quadruple wing-ding, landing on the candy floss stall and bouncing to a standstill right next to Billy and Ernesto.

It was Granny.

'What the . . . ?' said Old Bill, who was by this point more confused than an Eskimo in Ikea.

'What the . . . ?' said Ernesto, who was now more befuddled and bamboozled than a puppy in a tumble dryer.

'Who the . . . ?' said Billy, for obvious reasons.

'Your granny, that's who,' replied Granny. 'Now STOP HIM!'

Granny reached out a long, bony finger and pointed towards the exit of the Oh, Wow! Centre, in the direction of a shocking sight. Armitage! Tiptoeing away! His pockets spilling banknotes. A sack on his back bulging with booty.

Rudolph was close behind, still barking, with an exasperated expression on his face that seemed to mean, 'Finally! Are you all deaf or what?'

'What the . . . ?' said Old Bill, who was generally quite slow on the uptake and, as I'm sure you have already figured out, not particularly good at his job.

'How the . . . ?' said Ernesto, who now felt a glimmer of hope that justice might be done after all, but who was still too thrown by the sight of a granny doing a back somersault with a double pike, triple flip-flop and quadruple wing-ding to think straight.

'Come on!' said Billy, because thankfully at least

one person there had an alert mind and quick feet.

Billy set off and gave chase. Armitage continued to run away, dodging the security guards at the door of the centre, and beginning to circle the huge atrium. Old Bill joined the chase, followed by Ernesto, followed by Queenie, followed by Reginald Clench, who'd now come off stage, but was still dressed in a grass skirt and carrying a tuba.

While running at full speed, Clench gave three sharp tuba blasts on a high C sharp. A high C sharp on a tuba is a low C sharp on any other instrument, but, unless you have perfect pitch, that's not important right now. Three blasts of a tuba's high C sharp meant one thing. It was a message known to every member of the Ecstatic Aquatic Splashtastic Circus. An emergency message which meant, 'Rampage alert! Stop whatever you are doing, leave the sea lions and the piano tuna to entertain the audience, and come immediately.'

The whole cast obeyed the call and joined the chase: Jemima Steam, carrying three flaming torches and still steaming slightly from her rear end; Zygmond Tszyx and Zygmond Tszyvn, trailing a cloud of bubbles; Cissy Noodles and her now rather soggy poodles; the Aquabats of Arabia; Bunny Weasel and her momentarily unsynchronised otters; sundry sea-lion trainers, dolphin handlers, fish fanciers and sharkists;

and last of all Ruggles Pynchon, who had been halfway through a magic trick and was therefore invisible from the waist down.

All of them ran as fast as they could, one after the other, in a long, jumbled, drippy, bubbling, flaming, steaming, ottery line behind Reginald Clench, Queenie, Ernesto, the policeman with the wife with the dicky hip, Billy, Rudolph and Armitage.

This had not been Armitage's plan. He had been so close to sneaking away with all the loot, but now he was being chased by . . . he turned his head to check who was chasing him . . . and that sight is a vision that will haunt him until the end of his

days, or until he meets his dooooooom, whichever is sooner. Armitage was a man who had made plenty of narrow escapes in his time, but even though he was a good runner, a master of disguise, and a skilful slipper-away, right now he was in a serious pickle. He'd been chased before, but not like this.

He needed to think fast. That was a lot of people to shake off. And dogs. And otters.

At this point, the Oh, Wow! security guards, showing admirable skill in the art of crime prevention, noticed something was up and they gave chase too.

Armitage sprinted faster than he had ever run

before, still tailed by Rudolph, Billy, Old Bill, sundry mammals and fully-costumed circussers and a wheezy, out-of-breath gaggle of security guards. On and on the snake of chasers ran, gradually getting longer as various other people joined in. Soon, behind the criminal, his sort-of son, the policeman, the circussers, otters, poodles, marching Labrador and security guards were fifteen programme-sellers, twenty-one shop assistants, thirty-two walkie-talkie-holding people in high-visibility jackets, 🖤 forty-one passers-by who thought it was a game and four more dogs, just because dogs can't watch people run without joining in.

Walkie-talkie-holding people in high visibility-jackets appear from nowhere at all public gatherings. Nobody knows where they come from or where they go or what they are for.

It was a large atrium, which ran in a circle all the way round the auditorium. Armitage ran and ran, still clutching his sack of loot, chased by a line so long (a hundred and thirty-nine people, eleven dogs and six otters) that he now found himself running into the back of the last person who was running after him.

'Get out of my way,' snapped Armitage. 'Can't you seen I'm in a hurry?'

The slowest chaser stopped, turned, and saw that the person behind him was also the person who was supposed to be in front of him. It took a moment to figure out how this could have happened and, during this very same moment,

Armitage realised it was time for a Plan B.

He darted for the nearest emergency exit, rushed through, and jammed a broom into the door handles. As Plan Bs go, this one was pretty basic, but it would have to do.

The door buckled, heaved and creaked.

It didn't open.

The broom held.

For a creamy and delicious moment, Armitage thought he had got away.

But, as he turned to run for his getaway scooter, a cackle of triumph rising in his throat, something huge and curiously smelly loomed up in front of him. Narcissus. With a girl on his back. *That* girl. Hannah.

Armitage executed a neat swerve to run round the camel, but Narcissus executed an equally neat swerve, swerving into Armitage's swerve, knocking him off his feet.

Armitage splatted to the ground, just as the broom gave way and a hundred and fifty-six (mostly human) bodies tumbled out.

'Got you!' said Hannah.

If she had been the cackling sort, this would have been the perfect moment for a big, hearty, gloaty one. But that wasn't Hannah's style.

'Got you!' said Old Bill, who didn't have much imagination, so resorted to copying Hannah.

'I . . . I . . . I was just trying to put the money somewhere safe. There are bad people around,' stammered Armitage.

'Codswallop,' said Old Bill. This was one of his favourite words and he rarely had the opportunity to use it. 'You're nicked, good and proper, and no mistake.'

'You can use those handcuffs over there, can't you?' said Hannah, pointing downwards.

'I suppose I can,' replied Old Bill, unlocking Ernesto and slapping the cuffs onto Armitage's wrists.

Ernesto, his arms free, could now, at long last, hug his son. Never, in the extensive and cuddly history of hugs, can there ever have been an embrace as perfect as this one.

Within seconds, a hundred and thirty-nine people were weeping tears of pure joy, one person was weeping tears of frustration and self-pity, and a camel was beginning to feel peckish.

'This was all your doing, wasn't it?!' yelled Armitage, pointing a long, bony finger towards Queenie Bombazine, who was at that moment removing a shard of broken glass from her ear.

'Look in the sack, Armitage,' replied Queenie.

'Even if you had got away, it wouldn't have done you any good.'

Armitage glanced at the money spilling out of his sack and noticed, for the first time, something strange about the banknotes. Although they were the right colour, and although they did say £50 in the corner, they did not show the usual picture of the Queen with a crown on her head, nor did they bear the words, 'Bank of England'. These £50 notes were quite different. In the middle was a drawing of Armitage with a potty on his head and a kipper in his mouth, and at the top were the words 'Bank of You've Been Kippered'.

Even though Armitage already knew he'd been done like a kipper, this was a depressing sight. His kippering was even more comprehensive than he'd thought.

'It was a honeytrap,' said Queenie. 'And you walked right into it, like the greedy, good-for-nothing criminal you are.'

'YOU MARK MY WORDS!' snapped Armitage. 'I'll get you back one of these days! You'll pay for this! In money! Lots of it! You're not nearly as lovely as you think you are, Queenie Bombazine!'

'Oh, yes she is,' said Hannah.

'I think so, too,' said Granny.

'Lovely is the perfect word for it,' said Old Bill.

'Yup – she's definitely lovely,' said Ernesto.

'REALLY lovely,' chorused a hundred and thirty-five other voices.

'*Woofely*!' barked eleven dogs, which I think it is safe to assume was a canine vote of loveliness.

'*Squeak squeak squeak,*' squeaked the six synchronised otters (all at once, naturally). There's no way of proving what this meant, since otter squeaks are notoriously difficult to translate, but it's not hard to guess.

'SO WHAT!' yelped Armitage. 'Even if everyone does think you're lovely, I still don't like you, and one of these days I'm going to get you back.'

'For what?' said Queenie. 'For kippering you or for being lovelier than you?'

'Both. I hate being kippered and – yes! – I admit it. I'm jealous and I'm not ashamed of it and one of these days I'm going to be better than you, then you'll be jealous of me, so there!'

'Better than me at what?'

'Everything!'

'Right,' said Old Bill. 'We've heard more than enough from you. You're coming with me to the station.'

'YOU'LL NEVER PROVE ANYTHING,' ranted Armitage as he was dragged away. **'IT WASN'T EVEN REAL MONEY! IT'S HER YOU SHOULD BE GOING AFTER – SHE'S A SELF-CONFESSED FORGER! IF I THOUGHT IT WAS REAL MONEY, I NEVER WOULD HAVE TAKEN IT! WE WERE ONLY PLAYING! I'M AN** INNOCENT MAN! EVERYONE'S GOT IT IN FOR ME! MY MOTHER NEVER LOVED ME! I CAN'T WEAR PRISON CLOTHES, THEY'RE HIDEOUSLY UNFLATTERING! IF I GIVE YOU FREE TICKETS TO MY SHOW, WILL YOU LET ME GO? HOW ABOUT IF I LET YOU DRIVE MY ENORMOUS LORRY? TWICE? OK, I'LL LEND IT TO YOU FOR A WEEK.

A MONTH? A YEAR? OK, HAVE IT! HAVE THE LORRY! PLEASE! LET ME GO! PLEASE!'

TWENTY-TWO

A happy ending! How wonderful!
(Says who?)
Says me. And who are you, anyway?
(I'm the voice of doom. And I hate
happy endings.)
Well, go away!
(I don't want to.)
Go! You're not welcome here!
(Oh. OK. Bye then.)
Bye. That was weird.

O OFF ARMITAGE WENT, in handcuffs towards
the dismal fate he so richly deserved.

(Or did he?)

What's happening here? Is this happy ending

being derailed by devious, dastardly, doomy events? It can't be.

(It can.)

It can't.

(It can.)

You're back!

(I am.)

Oh, my goodness! Something is afoot. And not those lumps at the end of my legs. This is something else.

One last twist, one final shocking scheme, may be uncoiling itself before our very eyes. For who is that in the road up ahead of the police car, standing in the middle of the B764, waving her arms and stopping the oncoming vehicle? It is a woman, dressed rather scantily for this cool autumn evening. Next to her is a man who looks exceptionally French. And behind them is a lorry. Not a small lorry. Not even a medium-sized lorry.

An enormous lorry.

'Help us! Help! We're stranded! We've run out of petrol!' said the woman, pressing her hands into the bonnet of the police car, which had now stopped in front of her.

Old Bill stepped out of his car and examined the curious scene in front of him. He sensed there was something fishy (and also vaguely circussy) going on here, but, before he had the chance to figure out what that might be, Fingers O'Boyle leapt out from behind the enormous lorry and tied him up. Jesse (who was just finishing one of his longest ever sulks) lifted the tied-up policeman, carried him into a nearby field and, with a this-hurts-me-more-than-it-hurts-you expression on his face, tipped him upside down into a bush, a thorny bush, which, as things turned out, hurt the policeman far more than it hurt Jesse.

'Great work, people,' cackled Armitage, climbing out of the police car, free at last. Well, not really at last, since he'd only been under arrest approximately twenty minutes, but this felt like a long time to him, since being under arrest was right at the very top of Armitage's list of The Worst

Things That Can Ever Happen.

'It was me that thought of it,' said Hank and Frank, at the same time.

'No it wasn't, it was me,' said Frank and Hank, simultaneously.

'Me!'

'Me!'

'Me!'

'Me!'

While Hank and Frank hanked and franked, Fingers appeared with a length of rubber tubing

and siphoned the fuel out of the police car. Within a minute, the enormous lorry was back to its old self, roaring enormous, fume-belching roars, and carrying off Armitage Shank and his troupe, away from the policeman upside down in a thorn bush, away from the Oh, Wow! Centre, away from the middle of nowhere, towards further dastardly adventures, and no doubt towards a plan for some quite spectacular revenge.

TWENTY-THREE

Decision Time

AND THAT, MY PRETTIES, is more or less that. What more do you want? The shirt off my back? The shoes off my feet? The teeny tiny hairs in my ears?

So Armitage was on the run again (booooo!), while Billy was reunited with his father (hoorayyyy!), who had now realised that it might be a good idea to change out of his prison uniform. Granny was reunited with her grandson (yippeeeee!) and Hannah faced a big decision (hmmmmm). Did she want to stay with Queenie and join the circus? But if Queenie was going back into retirement, was there even a circus for her to join? Could she stay with Billy and Ernesto? But to go where and do what?

Before we get to her big decision, we have to tangle one last time with the puzzling puzzle that has puzzled her since the beginning of this tale. Who was her father? Armitage or Ernesto?

When she finally sat down with Ernesto, and he told her how he had come to marry Wendy, it ended up being a story that was full of answers, but not necessarily to the right questions. Hannah was horrified to hear that after the Cupcake Test, Wendy had in fact chosen Armitage. Ernesto thought this might have something to do with the fact that he had been sending her flowers every day for a month, not knowing that she hated flowers and was in fact allergic to them. He never found out why she at first rejected him, but he was heartbroken.

His heartbreak, however, only lasted until an extraordinary day a few months later when by a stroke of luck, the Espadrille and Shank circuses found themselves in Moscow at the same time. Wendy had burst into Ernesto's dressing room shortly before his show, in floods of tears. She'd just spotted Armitage stealing, and in an instant had realised that he wasn't a wonderful, charming, dashing, charismatic ringmaster, Svengali and entrepreneur, but was actually a stinky pig.

Wendy had looked up after relating her woeful story, with limpid, tear-filled eyes, and in that instant something amazing happened, something that felt a little bit like being lifted up by a tornado, zoomed around the entire planet, then dumped back down where you started, all in less time than it takes to blink. Yes, Ernesto and

Wendy fell in love.

Ernesto had been pining for her since long before the cruel day of the Cupcake Test, but in a magical instant, their love suddenly bloomed into something mutual, deep, and unshakeable. He knew straight away that she would leave Armitage and join his circus. 'The day after that, we got married,' he explained to Hannah, 'and we were so, so, so happy; and nine months later, you came along, which made us even happier, because you were simply the most exquisite, delicious, perfect little baby. But the trouble with being happy is that you tend to forget about the boring things in life, like money. I'd never been good at that stuff anyway, but I got worse than ever, and it wasn't long before we went broke and Shank took us over. So poor Wendy ran away from Armitage, only to find herself working for him again, and now he was meaner to her than to anyone else. It was Armitage that made us send you back to your granny. A year or so later, just after Billy was born, he forced us to take away the safety net. It was all my fault. If she'd never met me, she'd still be alive today.'

Ernesto burst into tears, and Hannah and Billy leapt towards him, holding him as tightly as their four arms could manage. He still seemed to be crying when they heard him say, 'I'm so happy to have you both back again. I'm happier than I've ever been. This is just the best thing that has ever happened. Joint top with that day in Moscow.'

A splutter now came out of his mouth that was either sobbing or laughter or both. It was hard to tell.

Emotions are strange things. At this moment, Ernesto's emotions seemed to be rather like an enormous lorry juggernauting at top speed down a motorway, while somehow also juggernauting in the opposite direction at the same time.

Hannah was still in Ernesto's powerful arms, wet with his tears and engulfed by his sob-laugh at the moment she asked if he really, a hundred per cent definitely was her father; but for some reason the question now felt less important than it had done only a short while ago.

He held her close, and responded in a sombre, intense voice. 'Like all the best trapeze artists, your mother was a quick thinker, and she changed her mind about things very fast. In Moscow, it took her about 0.03 seconds to fall in love with me. And this was only a day after she'd caught Armitage stealing and had fallen out of love with him.'

After hours of talking and crying and laughing and remembering and explaining and exploring and examining, at the end of it all, they decided, together, that the answer to this question didn't really matter after all. Hannah was Hannah. She was herself, no more no less, and nothing that had happened before she was born made any difference to who she was. Granny and Hannah and Billy and Ernesto and Hannah's other mother and father back home, they were family now. All of them. And exactly what kind of family they were, or how to explain it to other people, made no difference whatsoever. All that mattered was that they had found each other after a long and painful separation, and that they cared for one another, and that it was time for cake.

Since we have arrived at slices of cake all round, that can only mean one thing. This, quite clearly, is . . .

Except that . . .

a few questions . . .

. . . remain.

1. Where will Hannah go now?

2. Where will Ernesto and Billy go?

3. Will they all start a new circus together?

4. What will Armitage do next?

5. Revenge?

6. *You betcha.*

7. But betcha isn't a word and that isn't a question.

8. *And neither is that.*

9. And what is the longest river in Argentina?

CAN'T GET ENOUGH OF ARMITAGE SHANK AND HIS ROTTEN CIRCUS? THEN MAKE SURE TO LOOK OUT FOR...

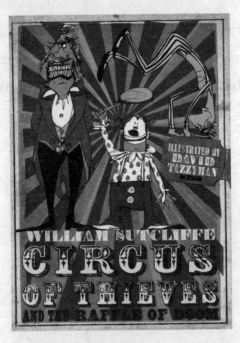